Watch
jogler
Lydia!

Hoo-hoo-hoo   "

RachaeLindsay   2013

A note from the author

Sometimes, in the night, when I can't sleep, I imagine other places.
And other worlds.
Do you?

Once, in real life, I went to Norway. I fell in love with the **craggy**
mountains and the **d**

e

e

p *fjords.*

My father and I met our first troll and, together, we wrote a poem about him which began:

" 'Midst Norway's craggy mountains
In a damp and gloomy cave
Sat hermit Hairy Bogley
Who wasn't very brave…"

And so it was that Hairy Bogley adopted me, tired of his damp home-cave. Now he sits on the warm hearth in the Snug.

But at night, when I am elsewhere in my mind, he bogles around the rest of the house.

He thinks I don't know.
But I do.

Hoo-hoo-hoo.

THE BOGLER'S APPRENTICE

RACHAEL LINDSAY

THE BOGLER'S APPRENTICE

Nightingale Books

NIGHTINGALE PAPERBACK

© Copyright 2008
Rachael Lindsay

A CIP catalogue record for this title is
available from the British Library

The troll-figurine on the cover page is an original Ny Form troll.
You will find all the Ny Form trolls at www.trollsofnorway.com

ISBN-13: 978 1 903491 72 0

Nightingale Books is an imprint of
Pegasus Elliot MacKenzie Publishers Ltd.
www.pegasuspublishers.com

First Published in 2008
Nightingale Books
Sheraton House Castle Park
Cambridge England
Printed & Bound in Great Britain

Dedication

Foor mi marvellurg, dearig Daddy, Neil Edney…
U leftig oos sadli.
U guarderig oos.
Gooshty nachtor.

Kissig, kissig.

Glossary

A

animor/es – animal/s
antoori - auntie

B

backen – back
badli - bad
baskettli – basket
biggy – big
bilbooren – bilberries
boot - boat
borg – bye
brekenfasht - breakfast
brushoori – brush
buzzors - bees

C

catchen – catching/to catch
choppen – (to) chop
clevor – clever
clinkoori – to clink ("cheers!")
comli – come/coming/to come

D

dearig – dear/dear one
dee - the
dedden – deadly/dangerous
dingle-donglor - bell
doggor – dog
dunder – (slang) dratted
dursty - thirsty

E

eatig – eat/eating/to eat
en – and
es – it's
excitig - exciting

F

fastli – faster
feelen - feeling
festli – feast
fetchen – fetching/to fetch/fetch(ed)
findor – will find/to find
fior - fire
fishen – fish/fishing/to fish
fixig – fixing/to fix
floweri/es – flower/s
foor – for
foresh - forest

G

gib – give(s)
goingor – going/to go
gooshty – good
guarderig – guarding/to be guarded

H

hab - have
halloo – hello
handlies – hands
happli - happy
helpen - help
herbie(s) – herb(s)
Herbie Poshtig – collecting pouch
                              (usually for herbs)
homerig - home
honig – honey
hor - how
hungeror – hungry

I

Im – I'm
Iv – I've

J

janglers - keys

K

kissig - kiss

L

leftig – left
liker - like
littelor – little
looki – look
lovelor - lovely
luckor - luck

M

marvellurg - marvellous
meer – me
mekken – making/to make
menor – men/people
mi - my
Mistig Vorter – Misty Water (Thom's boat)
moonish – moon
morgy - morning
morish - more
morsi(es) – mouse/mice
mushroomer – mushrooms
musten - must

N

nachtor – night/night-time
nay – no
needen – needing/to need
netsy - net
nics - not

O

onkli – uncle
oop - up
oos - us

P

painterig – paint
picken – picking/to pick
pleasor - please
poshtig – pocket
pussor - cat

Q

R

ropey – rope
rubbig – rub/to rub
runnig – run/to run

S

sadli - sad
scratchli – scratching/to scratch
seedlies – seeds
shtay – stay
shtop - stop
sitli – sit
soonig – soon
stoofid - stupid
strangeror - strange
strongish – strong

T

tay - tea
thingors – things
todagen – today
troddler – troll toddler

U

u - you
urnli - only

V

varken - wake
verisht – very
vildi - wild
visitori – visitor
vorter - water

W

wooden - wood
worrish/t – worries/d

X

Y

yo – yes

Z

Chapter One

he worn woodland path curled night-time fingers of mist over rocks and stone. When the wind rested from moaning for a moment and the treetops ceased waving, rustlings and scutterings of dark creatures could be heard as they ruffled leaves on the forest floor. The veil of the moon slipped in between black branches, flickering its cold light at his feet as he bogled along.

This was just how he liked it.

The forest full and fragrant.

Alone in his darkling world.

Secret.

Patting Herbie Poshtig at his side with one grimy hand, Hairy Bogley chortled to himself. It held more findings for his growing collection and he was looking forward to sorting them back in his cave.

Far below him, down through the depths of pine and spruce, the moon danced on shadowy lappings of the fjord. A boat bobbed gently against its moorings in the mist, waiting for the first light of day. The bee hives lay silent as the red-hooded figure slipped past, wet drips like dew gathering on the end of his bulbous nose, making him sniff.

The well-trodden path was familiar in the gloom and Hairy Bogley nodded as it took an upward turn towards overhanging ledges of rock. Flat-footed, he slapped his hairy feet on to steep steps and felt for guiding stones in the undergrowth with eager fingers. His troll tail followed.

Not far now.

Nearly home.

Beetles scuttled across his hands, alarmed at his intrusion, burrowing into heathers and mosses to escape. Step after step he climbed, until the upper ledge was reached at last. Hairy Bogley straightened his aching back and legs.

Down the steep bank, along the edge of the fjord, only a few lights twinkled from the houses of Big People. Most were sleeping soundly in their great beds. Doors were locked and windows closed tight; dogs were chained and snoring; cats were prowling through quiet streets looking for bins to raid and rats to catch. Children were dreaming of sunshine hours and playmates … or of *bogey-men* creeping from dark corners…

And there, hidden under hanging branches of birch and ash, the mouth of Bogley's home-cave welcomed him, grinning widely.

"Hoo-hoo-hoo!" he hooted quietly to himself as he clutched Herbie Poshtig, full of the night's spoils, and checking right and left to make absolutely sure he was alone, he slipped inside.

~~~

Hairy Bogley looked around with beady eyes and a childish smile on his old, whiskery face. He loved his secret hideaway and delighted in its nooks and crannies. Everything he needed was here, gathered from a life-time's night findings. His solitary life pleased him (his habits were not for polite company) and when he wished for troll friendship, he knew where to look. He had thought of taming a bat for a pet, but there again, their nocturnal habits were so similar that he would see nothing of his little friend. The sudden flare of a match cast a distorted silhouette on the rough walls as Bogley squatted to light the candles. He wiped the end of his nose and scratched his round belly, which rumbled thunderingly in the silence.

...a distorted silhouette...as Bogley squatted to light the candles

"Nachtor festli foor meer," he muttered to himself in his native Troll Talk, as he sniffed. "Im verisht hungeror!"

Having set the candles on ledges and in chiselled holes and hung up his hood on a peg, Hairy Bogley looked around for Herbie Poshtig, his faithful leather pouch which accompanied him on all his expeditions. The pouch was traditionally made and held on a strong, wide shoulder strap to allow the owner free hands for gathering. Usually herbs were picked from their wild homes in the forest – selected fresh and aromatic for soup, troll medicines and their air-sweetening properties when hung from rafters and beams. Hairy Bogley's Herbie Poshtig however, was used for an altogether different purpose.

Poking out from the top was a cooked hen's leg. It was scrawny and had little left on it, but it was a real midnight feast for a hungry troll. Bogley pulled it from the pouch and began to gnaw. His gappy front teeth tugged at the stringy meat, tough as it was, and he slurped his tongue round the end of the bone. When it was clean and bare, Bogley tipped his head to one side and, using all the strength of his grinders, he crunched away at the splinters until everything was demolished.

"Marvell*urg*!" he exclaimed, burping the "urg" and wiping his greasy mouth on the back of his gritty hand.

Cake came next: a great big chunk of dry stodge which he snatched out of Herbie Poshtig and stuffed into his mouth. It took some time to chew. It crumbled into a sort of sawdust and he quickly ran out of spit, which wasn't like Bogley. Cheeks bulging, he looked around his home for a drink and found an old chipped mug of mountain water, collected the previous week. Some dribbled down his chin as he tried to squeeze it in, but he had enough to change the sawdust into a thick, claggy paste which he could swallow in one big clod. More gulped water and he was done.

The night air was chill, and now that Bogley had satisfied his hunger, he realised that he had not yet lit the fire. Quickly he gathered twiggy sticks from a corner and piled them like a magpie's nest in the centre of the cave. They were dry and soon caught, sending sparks and crackles swirling upwards in a fug of choking smoke. Hairy Bogley rubbed his hands together and held them against the flames. Thicker branches were carefully criss-crossed over the top and began to glow deep ambers and reds. The colours filled his home with a rosy cosiness, adding a flickering light to the candles. Rough and ready as it was, it had to be the perfect place for Hairy Bogley.

His home.

His home-cave.

His own.

Alone.

Crouching down by the warming fire, a scratchy blanket covering his shoulders, Bogley began to unpack Herbie Poshtig. Somewhere outside, an owl hooted.

"Hoo-hoo-hoo!" echoed the troll as he reached inside the pouch. This was his favourite part of the night. Expedition over, full belly, crackling fire and time to sort his findings. Sniffing loudly, he pulled out the first of his collection.

It had stiff brushed whiskers, much straighter and darker than his own; thick and glossy, all in a line. The whiskers were packed tightly into a metal band which then grew into a wooden handle. Bogley turned the object this way and that, his great grimy hands gentle, with curious fingers.

"Verisht strangeror," he murmured to himself. He considered poking the fire with the handle but realised, just in time, that it was not very long and he would get perilously close to the flames – and that it was, indeed, made of wood and so not the best poker to use. He flicked the bristles wonderingly with his thumb and watched how they shifted back into their soldier-straight line. Cautiously, he sniffed it and in so doing, the whiskers of the strange object brushed against his own white, wiry ones. It made his nose tickle and he rubbed it furiously with the dirty palm of one hand. It smelled of the sheds and outbuildings he visited so often where the Big People lived. It was a strong breath-catching smell, which reminded him of some of the bottles and jars he sometimes came across. Then a slow smile grew upon Hairy Bogley's face. He knew what he could use this for!

Perfect for sweeping back the whiskers on his face and tidying up the shock of wispy hair which stuck out so wildly around his ears! With swift movements, he held the wooden handle and brushed backwards and forwards in excitement, his grubby face turned upwards to the roof of his cave.

Placing his special whisker brush down on the dusty floor, Bogley reached once more inside Herbie Poshtig. Out came his next finding. It was cold and hard. It felt heavy in his hand. The long cylinder was made of a shiny metal which glinted in the firelight. One end belled out and had a flat smooth window, round and clear. Inside was a small sphere but it was impossible to touch it, tucked away as it was. Once more, the troll turned it over in his hands. This really was a mystery.

"Biggy Menor hab excitig thingors!" Bogley exclaimed in the firelight.

On one side of the cylinder was a small jutting out piece. Just the one. Absent-mindedly, he rubbed his thumb over it. He could feel tiny, rough ridges across it, perhaps for a better grip. Maybe he should hold this part more tightly; he knew that ropes which were rough were much easier to hang on to than smooth ones. And the rocky steps outside his home-cave were slippery when smooth, but easy to bogle down when they had ruts carved into them.

"Hmmm," he wondered out loud.

Holding the length of the metal case in his hand, he increased his grip so that his thumb pushed against the ridged piece. A quiet click was heard and

- in an instant - the cave was flooded with a bright light!

Hairy Bogley leapt to his feet in fright and dropped his find in alarm. The bright light fell away from the cave walls and shone from the window end in a wide triangle over the stone floor. The troll edged cautiously towards it. He nudged it with one flat foot. The light rolled to shine out through the entrance of the cave. Branches of pine and sleepy birds in their nests could be seen quite clearly, blinking in the unexpected dawn which shone upon them, the moon having long since dropped from the sky. Bogley poked at the light on the floor of the cave. A great finger shadow stretched out before him. He grinned his best bogley grin. He knew all about shadows in the night.

"Im clevor troll! Im catchen dee moonish!"

Picking up his moon-stick, he shone it around his home, delighting in its brightness and searching out the darkest of corners. He practised turning the moon on and off with the switch. He made shadow puppets on the walls, having troll conversations with each character he saw. Then the light shone on Herbie Poshtig and reminded Hairy Bogley that other findings were awaiting him.

Just two more left. Which one to choose? He delved into the pouch and rummaged around. Out came a long, thin, metal stick, again with a handle of wood. The handle this time was shaped like the pears which grew on the lower slopes near the fjord edge. It was smooth and rounded, feeling good in the palm of the troll's rough hand. The metal stick had a flattened, straight-edged end. Bogley remembered when he found this one there had been a few, all similar in shape but different in size. Having a choice meant that he had selected the largest, of course; Bogley always thought that BIG was BEST. As he pondered about its use, he reached over his left shoulder and began to scratch his back. Left a bit, right a bit, up a bit – no, too far – down a bit. Just there!

Of course! A back-scratcher!

So that's why they came in different sizes: for different sizes of backs!

"Yo, yo, Bogley," he chortled as he scratched, "backen scratchli!" What a useful find that one was! As he placed it carefully with the others he thought he could also use it for stirring soup, if he ever made any…

And so, as the first pale hints of dawn began to creep over the inky water below his cave, the last finding of the night was retrieved from Herbie Poshtig. Hairy Bogley knew what these were. He had seen them many a time dangling from doors of houses and sheds, hung on hooks and left under plant pots. They were used to make it easy or hard to enter or escape from a Big Person's house. Sometimes they turned quietly; sometimes they jammed and clunked. Trolls didn't have any use for them as they used catches and bolts when necessary.

These were a bit different, though. They had a piece of leather attached which bore some marks. Hairy Bogley gazed at them inquisitively:

DYNO-TRUK

The lines on the leather meant nothing to him and he certainly didn't have a door to the cave to try them in, but the way they jangled as he shook them pleased him. He held them up to hear them more clearly. Then, hooking them over his ear to listen to them as he moved, he jiggled his head from side to side. To his delight, they stayed in place.

"Looki!" he shouted in his cave. "Nay handlies!" and he danced about the dying embers of his fire until the smoke swirled so much he had to stop and cough and cough and cough.

~~~

Yellow cloudberries embraced the first rays of morning sunshine, glistening with droplets of mountain dew. A badger snuffled its way back to its sett after a night-time's foraging for worms and fallen fruit. Partridges began to peck-peck for seeds in the fields below. Daytime animals awoke to greet the new morning as flowers uncurled smiling petal faces.

Hairy Bogley saw all this, rubbed his eyes, and knew it was time for bed. He gathered up his findings and carried them to the back of his home-cave. Sitting on his haunches, he lifted a heavy, flat stone to reveal a large hole beneath. In went the whisker-brusher and the moon-stick. In went the back-scratcher and the door-janglers.

Safe.

Secret.

To use sometime, because you never could tell...

Hairy Bogley, yawning now with a great, gaping, gappy-toothed groan, wrapped himself up in his old blanket. As he lay by the dimming fire glow, he sighed. This had been a good night. An exciting night. A fun night.

"Hoo-hoo-hoo," he murmured, as he fell into a heavy sleep.

~~~

Chapter Two

rimo, the smoky-grey cat, stretched himself in the late morning sunshine and rested his chin on his paws in purring satisfaction. His favourite smoked fish for breakfast and a warm window ledge to snooze on. What could be better? He considered his plans for the day:

1. Lick his paws and whiskers.

2. Sun himself.

3. Sleep.

4. Stretch a little.

5. Sleep.

6. Stretch, yawn and check the weather. If cloudy, go inside on to Hildi and Thom's bed. If still sunny, find some shade in the forest to sit. And think.

7. Chew a bit of grass. Maybe.

8. Check out the mice. Hopefully bash them a bit.

9. Supper-time.

10. Bed.

All in all, a pretty hectic schedule he thought, sighing, as he began to clean left-over fish from his beautiful whiskers. Living with the trolls, Hildi and Thom, in the middle of the forest was a good life for Grimo. Tracker, their dog, was a bit of a worry now and then but soon sorted out with a combination of cat's claws and dog's nose. Tracker had adopted Thom many months before and had a history of unfortunate experiences, as far as Grimo could make out. This meant he would do anything for a kind word and adored the gentle trolls. In fact, he was utterly devoted to them which made Grimo feel rather superior. But what could anyone expect? After all, thought the cat, he was a *dog.* The sun shone on Grimo strongly, making his eyes glazed and lazy. Soon his paws were twitching as he caught dream mice in a far-away land.

~~~

Hildi hummed a troll tune as she set her basket on the kitchen table. Thom had long since left, with Tracker at his heels, taking long strides downhill towards the fjord. The dog followed eagerly, nose to the ground as always, keeping just behind Thom's troll tail which trailed a little on the forest path. Two mice were watching Hildi from their position on the dresser.

"Where do you think she's going, Scratchen?" Tailo asked, thoughtfully rubbing his fat, brown tummy. "Any chance of bilberries today, do you think? Or cranberries even?"

"You're not hungry already are you, fat Rat-Face?" replied his brother incredulously. "You've only just finished that porridge stuff!"

Tailo tut-tutted his yellow teeth and shook his head as if the other mouse was really rather stupid.

"A mouse of my Splendid Physique and Physical Splendour needs vitamins! Especially ones from fresh, luscious fruit - plenty of them too! Mouse can not live on oats alone, you know. Haven't you heard the 5-a-day rule?"

Scratchen had stopped listening, too busy scritch-scratching round his neck and ears. He was well-used to Tailo's greed and grand statements. Ever since they had arrived on a ship and scampered through the forest to Hildi and Thom's door, they had lived in relative luxury but Tailo didn't seem to appreciate it. It had been difficult to understand the trolls at first, but their acceptance of Tailo's cantankerous ways, Scratchen's kick-kicking habits and the ready availability of food had meant that the mice stayed as long-term guests.

Hildi cast a glance up at the mice in response to their squeaking.

"Yo, yo, morsies!" she laughed. "Im goingor in foresh foor mushroomer. Bilbooren picken. Herbies..." Her voice trailed off as she reached for her headscarf and tied it over her wispy white hair, patting it in place and straightening her simple shift dress. She still missed the ancient beads from around her neck which used to glint in the sunbeams streaming through the old kitchen window, flashing coloured light around the room. The thought made her hesitate for a moment to check all was well.

There was no noise.

No Big Men coming to the door with great bangings. Nobody to surprise them. Nobody to demand anything from them. Nobody to knock her to the floor, like before, and threaten their peaceful lives….

She shook her head to clear the bad memories. She checked that the cuckoo clock was wound up and safely latched to protect the Troll Treasure map.

All was well.

Hildi blinked to clear her eyes of the sudden tears which had formed and smiled bravely at the watching mice.

"Morsies? In baskettli pleasor!"

The mice didn't need to be asked twice. With excited squeaks, they scrambled down the dresser and on to the floor, up the sturdy table leg and scrabbled into the basket. Tailo was last as usual. He always made out that it was because of his impeccable manners he let the thinner, scrawnier Scratchen go first, but really it was because of his roundness and the fact that he got so out of breath so quickly.

Scooping the basket on to one arm and hanging her Herbie Poshtig over the other shoulder, Hildi opened the door of their little dwelling. The forest lay ahead, bathed in a green glow and the promise of tasty mushrooms, juicy fruit and sweet-scented herbs.

~~~

The drowsy hum of the hives greeted Thom as he arrived in the sunny clearing. Honey bees buzzed in a heady heather scent nearby, gathering sweet nectar in their sacs. Tracker gave a little whimper and dropped down low when he saw where Thom was. This was *not* his favourite place. Bees were tricky at the best of times and he didn't intend to go any closer. He rubbed the end of his wet nose with one great paw in sympathetic memory and turned mournful eyes towards his beloved master.

"Nay worrish,Tracker!" Thom reassured him. "Sitli en shtay. Gooshty doggor!"

Tracker understood completely. He didn't intend to do anything else, actually! Thom set down a small bucket amongst the flowers and took out a bundle of clothing. Carefully he donned the protective hat and veil which shielded him from possible stings.

They almost smothered him, the hat coming right down over his eyes, making it difficult to see the hives and where he was going. Then he pulled on huge gloves which made him feel awkward and clumsy. Hildi had got this outfit for him when she exchanged some of her beautiful forest pictures with the Big People. Thom hadn't the heart to tell her that the clothes were far too big, as Hildi was so concerned for his welfare and she had been so excited with her gift.

The honey bees were lazy today. It was nearing the end of a warm summer; almost all the honeycomb cells were filled and the last were being sealed with beeswax. The swarm had grown with the hatching of young bees and the queen was getting old. Thom knew that he would have to split the colony and move them to a new skep soon.

Not just yet, though. Honey to harvest!

Tracker looked down the path into the clearing, watching Thom as he lifted oozing, sticky pieces of honeycomb and placed them with care into his honey bucket. The dog licked his lips and rested his head sorrowfully on his paws, wishing he could taste just a little bit.

~~~

Hildi's basket swung on her arm as she wandered through the forest. There were many fine mushrooms hiding in shady, damp clefts amongst trees and leaves, but she picked only the freshest and those she knew were safe to eat. Many, many years ago Hildi had been taught the art of mushroom-picking, when as a young troll she had followed in her mother's footsteps. She still remembered the rules:

"Nics verisht biggy,

Nics verisht littelor,

Urnli foor eatig,

Leftig gib gooshty luckor!"

Hildi, like all trolls, was keen not to disturb the natural ways of the forest. She knew the fungi were part of an important cycle and would pick only as many as she needed to eat. If she respected the life around her, plants and animals would thrive and she and Thom could live in harmony with them. She also believed it would bring them good luck, for many fae creatures shared the forest, living amongst the toadstools and mushrooms. All trolls knew it was very unwise to upset *them*!

Tailo and Scratchen scrambled out of the basket when it was set down and scampered off into the undergrowth. This was always a good time for foraging for fallen nuts and berries, because Hildi was so slow and meticulous in her mushroom-picking. Occasionally, the mice would find what they thought was a fine specimen for her and squeak loudly to draw the troll's attention to it. Sometimes, Hildi was pleased and would break the mushroom gently away from its base. Sometimes, though, Hildi would draw a sudden shocked breath and cry:

"Nay morsies! Nics gooshty mushroomer! Verisht dedden! Nay, nay – shoo, shoo!" as she shooed the frightened pets away.

Tailo could never understand the fuss. One mushroom looked much the same as any other to him. How could one be good to eat and yet another so deadly? There was more to this mushroom-picking than met the eye, he decided, and thought he was better off concentrating on finding his own food.

~~~

Tracker suddenly lifted his head from his paws and sniffed the air. His dreamy eyes became alert and his ears pricked up.

What was that?

Who else was in the forest today?

The sunny glade where Thom was collecting honeycomb was quiet apart from the lazy drone of the bees, but there had been a strange noise. He was sure.

The dog's hackles rose as his sharp eyes searched the forest path behind him for a glimpse of whom or whatever it was.

Nothing seemed changed. All was still.

Again Tracker sniffed the air, unconvinced that they were alone. The dog's lips curled back from his teeth and he gave a low growl. Thom heard this and immediately looked up from his work.

"Tracker?" he queried. "U guarderig?"

Thom also glanced down the path which led back into the forest, but could see nothing different.

"Strangeror..." he murmured and then shook his troll head and smiled. "Gooshty guarderig doggor! Iv fetchen honig. Im goingor homerig, Tracker." And, clicking his tongue in encouragement, he picked up his honey bucket, full of golden sweetness, and started back for home.

~~~

By now Grimo had licked his paws and whiskers, sunned himself, slept, stretched, slept some more, stretched again, yawned and checked the weather. The sun was lower in the sky, but it was still warm. The cat thought through his check list. Now where was he up to? Slowly he got to his paws and stretched a long, low, back-arched stretch. Hmmm. Next? Ah, yes!

Shade - and mice!

Now where were they?

The cat jumped nimbly down from his window ledge bed and strolled down the path which led from the troll dwelling into the shade of the forest, pausing only to chew on a blade of grass. Afternoon sunlight glinted on his smoky-grey stripes showing them silver and sleek.

"Littelor morsies!" he purred. "Im comli!"

Grimo knew which path Hildi usually took when mushroom-picking and he also knew the short cuts. Over time, he knew every centimetre of these well-worn paths: the smells, the animals that had passed that way, the texture of the earth beneath his paws. All of it was very familiar and safe to this cat.

Until.

A rut.

A new rut in the path, just where it widened.

There was a digging in of the ground, smooth and with a clear-cut edge. And then another. And another. Regularly spaced on the bend in the forest. Until the soft mud hardened and the ruts were no more.

Grimo felt a little uneasy. Something had left a track which didn't smell of animal. Then it had disappeared into the forest.

Sharp squeaking brought his thoughts back to the here and now. Tailo and Scratchen were nearby and they were giving the game away with excited noises.

"Scratchen – cranberries! Lookie here! Come quickly!"

Tailo's urgent cries of greed reached Scratchen's ears and he hurried over. There were a few cranberries (usually found in the valley) here in the wood! The two mice fell upon them and popped each one like a balloon with their pointed, yellow teeth. Juice burst into their mouths and ran through their whiskers.

"Oh wow!" exclaimed Scratchen in a full-mouth sort of way. "These are sooooo wonderf - "

but he was cut off, mid-delight, by a dreadful screech from Tailo.

That Cat was upon them!

Grimo had leapt out from his hidey-hole and, with a practised bash of his paw, had swept Tailo off his feet into the air. Scratchen scurried for cover at the base of a nearby spruce, gulping the last gobbets of cranberry juice, coughing and spluttering. Tailo landed with a dull thud, all air knocked from him, on his back, little legs akimbo. Scratchen squawked as loudly as he could for Hildi's help.

Tailo landed…on his back, little legs akimbo

"Yo, yo, Scratchen!" she replied, arranging her last piece of wild garlic alongside the angelica in her Herbie Poshtig. Mushrooms were laid in the basket and now the herbs she needed were gathered as well.

"Now, Mrs Troll!" yelled the little black mouse in desperation. "HELP!"

Hildi looked up from her gatherings to see a determined cat stalking Scratchen and fat, little Tailo flat on his back amongst the pine needles on the forest floor.

"GRIMO! NAY!" she shouted in horror, flinging her basket to the ground. "Badli pussor!"

Grimo stopped in his stalking tracks, one paw raised, head suddenly turned to his mistress. Hildi was approaching in a very meaningful way. He sat down hurriedly and licked the fur at his side, with as much an air of innocence as he could muster.

Hildi ignored him and scooped up the two mice, returning them to the safety of the basket where Tailo collapsed into the earthy smell of fresh mushrooms. He winced as he fell, but gave a great sigh of relief.

Mouse: 1   Cat: 0

Hah!

~~~

Leaving the honey bucket in the middle of the table in their little kitchen, Thom decided that there were still enough daylight hours to go down to the fjord to check on Mistig Vorter and busy himself with boat-type jobs; something he loved to do. Tracker had lol-lupped great gulps of water from the stream outside and was ready to join him, tail wagging and ears pricked. Hildi had just returned from the forest and was eager to set out her mushrooms and herbs, planning to hang the wild garlic from a corner of the low ceiling. She wanted to make soup and scrape the pieces of honeycomb to release the heather-fragrant amber into her special honey pots. The mice, exhausted after their Nasty Experience, were curled round each other on the top of the dresser, tucking their heads well down into their furry chests.

"Im goingor Mistig Vorter, Hildi," Thom called as he padded to the door. "Backen foor tay. Gooshty borg!"

Hildi smiled. She was happy to have the place to herself just now. Thom would only get under her troll feet. Mice quiet. Cat and dog out. Perfect!

The early evening sun was beginning to glow pink by the time Thom reached his little boat. Mistig Vorter bobbed its usual greeting, keen to be taken out further on to the water.

"Nachtor soonig, mi lovelor boot. Nay fishen todagen!" Thom murmured as he patted the bow. As he did so, his hairy hand felt some rough paint which flaked off and fell into the water. Blue on blue. The troll frowned slightly and looked along the side of his little craft, noticing other areas needing attention.

"Halloo, Thom!"

A shout made him look up in surprise. Tracker leapt to his feet and barked two sharp barks.

In the distance, dangling dirty feet in the icy water of the fjord and sitting on a rock, grinning toothily, was Hairy Bogley. He was waiting for the sun to go down. Thom gave a yell of delight and waved his arms in greeting, beckoning his old friend over. With a splash, Bogley jumped off his perch and waded along to Mistig Vorter. The two trolls solemnly gripped hands and bent foreheads to touch in traditional greeting before slapping each other on the back and hugging. Tracker danced around them, yelping excitedly and jumping up to lick.

"Nay! Nay, Tracker!" Thom exclaimed, wiping his face. "Sitli! Sitli!"

It had been a few seasons since Thom and Bogley had last met. It didn't happen very often, which had always puzzled Thom. They never seemed to bump into each other in the forest, or on the mountain paths, or by the bee hives, or indeed at the edge of the fjord. They never saw him in a boat, enjoying the cold, crisp sunshine of winter, or paddling hairy feet during the warm days of summer, or collecting berries in autumn or delighting in new spring growth on the hillsides. Hildi and Thom had often wondered how Hairy spent his time. He was a bit of an odd one.

After warmly greeting each other, the two sat down to talk. Thom pointed to the peeling paint on the side of his precious boat.

"Im needen painterig en brushoori," Thom smiled sadly, knowing that it would be difficult to get these without a trip to the Big People, which he didn't look forward to. The trolls always tried to be self-sufficient, living as they did on the mountainsides and in the forest. Only when they needed something they really couldn't make themselves or find, did they consider exchanging some of Hildi's beautiful forest or water pictures. Money didn't exist for them. There had been one occasion when Thom had attempted to trade for money, but it had almost led to such disaster that Thom had vowed never to think of such a plan again.

Hairy Bogley scratched his whiskery chin and looked thoughtful.

"Brushoori," he mused, taking off his red hood and sweeping his wild hair away from his face. He might have just the thing, back in his home-cave…

That night, as Hildi and Thom sat in front of their little fire, mice snoring sweetly, a brand new paintbrush was placed silently on their doorstep.

~~~

Chapter Three

he moon had begun to wane; it was no longer full like the night before. It shone with a milky glow through some gathering clouds. The evening was chill and Hairy Bogley felt the whiskery hairs on the back of his neck prickle. It was not cold enough to grow the troll fur of winter yet, but he needed to draw his red hood down over his large ears to keep them warm as he bogled along, flat feet sure and silent.

He paused, squatting on a rock to look far below him, down the mountainside. The lights of the big houses were gradually beginning to go out as the Big People yawned, stretched, put out the cats, chained up the dogs and went to bed. The yellow night-eyes of the town winked and blinked shut until nearly all was dark.

"Fetchen painterig foor Thom," the troll muttered to himself as he gazed into the blackness. "Hmmm," he wondered, scratching his chin.

After scraping the last few crumbs of dry cake from the bottom of Herbie Poshtig, Hairy wiped his mouth on the back of his sleeve and slowly stood up. Jacket buttons fastened securely against the mountain air and baggy trousers pulled well up to his armpits, he began his descent.

Finding and collecting from the Big People had kept Bogley amused ever since he was a young troll. Indeed it had become essential for his survival at times when he had no food in his home-cave or he needed blankets for warmth. He was a loner. He had lived all his life tucked away up the mountainside, comfortable with his habits. He had troll friends of course, who always welcomed him as one of their own with the usual troll hospitality, but by choice Hairy lived by himself. So long had he lived like this that he could no longer remember his troll parents or family, and very little about being young. He had been an old hermit all his life, it seemed. Other trolls in the forest could not really understand why he chose to live like this and never really knew how he managed. All they did know was that every now and then there would be an extra mouth to feed at the table and a useful gift left.

That night, Hairy Bogley had his moon-stick with him for the first time. It flickered over the woodland path and darted in and out of the black trees. He grinned as he played with its light, startling owls and flashing up at the bats which swooped overhead. On and on he padded. As he turned a familiar corner nearing the edge of the forest though, the troll suddenly stopped. Something was different here.

The path was different.

It felt rougher and more rutted to his feet.

Regularly spaced grooves.

And the trees seemed thinner. Some of the branches were missing, making them look skeletal amongst the others.

And the path was altogether just that bit wider.

Hairy Bogley stood absolutely still, listening. Nothing was to be heard apart from the distant chime of the town church clock as it registered the half hour. There were no familiar hoots of owls just here. The bats were flying high further up the mountainside. Not just here. As they usually did.

Something was not quite right in this part of the forest.

~~~

Grimo was on a night hunt. Hildi and Thom had long since settled Tracker on the rug by the fire and the mice were munching nuts and berries in their sleep on the dresser. They knew they were safe from That Cat as long as they were in the trolls' home. They were all one family inside. Grimo licked his pretty lips with the tip of his pink tongue as he thought of Tailo and Scratchen. *Outside* though was a different matter. When they were outside in the forest, they were fair game and it was always worth keeping an eye on their movements. At any time during the day they might decide to stretch their scuttering legs or join Hildi on a walk to gather herbs. Tonight however was a night for the forest mice, with their beady little eyes and twitchy noses, their licorice tails and crunchy parts. The cat's mouth watered as he stalked off into the inky blackness.

~~~

Quite satisfied that he was alone, Hairy Bogley cast a last glance back down the path he had trodden and, switching off his moon-stick, set foot on to the hardened paving of the town's street. His hairy feet made no sound and his tail was well tucked into the back of his trousers. He kept to the shadows as much as he could in case a Big Person should see him and think it a curious sight. He also wanted to avoid any dogs that were free of kennels and chains. He knew his trollness had a unique scent which made him easy to follow. His heart beat fast and he kept eyes and ears alert for signs of danger. Trolls were a source of both amusement and fear amongst the Big People. Some thought trolls were to be ridiculed as strange forest-dwellers, with short legs and dangling tails. Some were superstitious about them, thinking they would be the bringers of misfortune and so were to be sought out. He had overheard talk of troll hunts and planned capture from time to time. It made all trolls shudder. It was safe to venture so close to the town only under cover of darkness, unless a troll had a really good reason to visit. He knew that Hildi exchanged some of her glorious forest or fjord pictures for essentials from time to time, with trusted townspeople at arranged meeting places. He, like all the trolls in the region, knew of Thom's visit to Bergen and the danger he had put himself in. Hairy did not doubt the need for caution, even at night.

The shed which had held the whisker brush the night before stood next to the door of the Big People's house. It was largely in darkness although a small light remained in the upstairs window and it was enough to show his shadow if he crept any closer. Enticingly, the old shed door was slightly ajar, unlike on the previous visit. Hairy sat back on his haunches in the blackness to weigh this up.

"Verisht strangeror," he thought to himself. He knew from experience that Big People were very fussy about shutting doors of out-houses, sheds and their homes at night. They were usually locked or latched or bolted. Unlike trolls, whose homes were always open to each other, Big People didn't trust other Big People.

Especially at night.

This particular shed had been latched shut when Bogley had last paid a visit. It had been in complete darkness too. He had been able to slip the strap from Herbie Poshtig underneath the latch and pull with all his weight against it until it had given way, opening the door with a sudden whoosh, making him tumble into the bushes nearby. It had been fairly easy to get in then and collect his findings.

But not *this* easy.

~~~

The cat's footfalls could barely be heard, so silent was he as he picked his way through the undergrowth. A rustle made him suddenly motionless, except for the twitching of his nose. Hedgehog or mouse? Grimo couldn't be sure; the scent of pine was so strong in this part of the forest. He had to be certain. He had battled with the spiky variety before now and it hadn't been good. Cautiously, he lowered his raised paw so that he could cower down in the blueberry bushes, ears flat, tail outstretched behind him.

Another rustle made the cat flinch and place his head flat on the ground, eyes round and saucerish, muscles tensed and ready to spring. A scratch of fallen pine needles to his left made Grimo flick round and he darted, claws unsheathed and gleaming, ready for the kill –

but the brown hare landed a breath-thumping blow with her great back feet. She caught Grimo squarely in the ribs, sending him flailing backwards into the undergrowth. Fur raised, the cat screeched wildly and was left wheezing and coughing as the hare bounded out of sight.

~~~

Hairy Bogley decided it had to be a trap. The small light still on in the window above, the shed door being left slightly open as if to invite a collector of findings. Carefully, he clicked the switch of his moon-stick and shone a thin beam of light on to the door. It certainly wasn't open much. Perhaps it had been a careless mistake after all. Perhaps the Big People just hadn't latched it securely enough that night. Then the thin beam caught sight of something else. Just at the top of the door, faintly shining, was a dangling cone. It hung down with a bronze clapper inside it.

Hairy Bogley quietly switched off his moon-stick and smiled broadly. "Dingle-donglor!" he breathed to himself. He knew all about *them*! He had dealt with these before and this was no match for an experienced bogler like him! It just made bogling even more fun!

The bell had to be muffled. How to reach it though? The troll looked about him in the gloom. After years of practice, his eyes were well-accustomed to working in the dark and he soon spotted a wheel barrow propped up against the garden fence. Hairy padded over to it and took it in his grimy hands. The wheel was not quite straight on its axle so it squeaked slightly, which was a worry, but within two squeaks the barrow was in position underneath the bell. Silently, Bogley climbed on and, by balancing on his tippest of toes, he found he could reach. With deft fingers, the clapper was unhooked from inside and slipped into Herbie Poshtig. One quick glance up at the lit window was all it took for the troll to jump down off the barrow, open the shed door - without a dingle or a dongle - and he was inside!

All sorts of objects were packed on shelves and in higgledy-piggledy corners. There were tools which towered menacingly over Hairy Bogley, their sharp points and rakish heads spear-like in the darkness. There were boxes overflowing with old cloths and brushes, empty jam jars and bottles with rusting lids destined never to be used. Two large wheels rested against one wooden wall, bent and with spikes poking out. A roll of wire was lying on the floor.

"Strongish ropey!" Hairy murmured as he looped it over one arm. "Gooshty foor fixig thingors."

By the light of his moon-stick, he could see paper packets with pictures of flowers and vegetables, scattered on an old table next to pots and a small earthy mound. As he handled them, they shook interestingly. Into Herbie Poshtig with those!

Hairy sniffed the damp air of the musty surroundings. He recognised the strong, breath-catching smell he associated with his whisker brush and began to search for what might be paint. The smell seemed to come from some tins stacked at the back of the shed. He shone his moon-stick on them.

They had hardened dribbles of colour down the side and as Hairy lifted them he could tell from the weight that some held more than others.

It was just as he was trying to decide which one to select that he heard a shout:

"Quick! Quick! The wheelbarrow's been put by the shed! Did you leave it there?"

The shed window was suddenly bright as lights were thrown on in the Big Person's house. Hairy Bogley had no time to lose. Forgetting all cares as to paint colour and quantity, he lunged at the nearest tin and, wire looped over one arm and Herbie Poshtig slung over his shoulder, he flung open the shed door and fled into the night.

~~~

A slow drizzle began to fall in the forest. Grimo scowled up at the sky which was beginning to soften from black into charcoal. No mice tonight then. It was time to curl up on Hildi and Thom's patchwork cover and sleep. His side felt bruised and sore from the hare's kicking and his grey stripes were becoming damp. With an irritable lash of his tail, the cat wound his way through the trees homewards. He nearly got that hare. If only he had been just that bit *quicker*. If only the hare had been just that bit *slower*. If only his claws had been just that bit *sharper*. Grimo stopped to examine his front paws. His claws weren't quite as razor-like as he would wish. It could make just the difference next time.

A fallen tree lay across the path in front of him. It made the cat stop and consider. It was certainly an excellent scratching post. At full stretch, he gripped the bark with ten needles, ears well back.

Snig-snag! Snig-snag! Snig-snag!

Tiny sawdust bits flew about him as Grimo sharpened busily. In excitement he darted round the tree trunk, dashing wildly and changing direction giddily. Then, just as suddenly, he stopped.

There was rather a lot of sawdust actually. In piles on the forest floor next to the fallen tree. This tree had not just fallen. And looking around him, Grimo could see it wasn't the only one.

How very odd.

~~~

Hairy Bogley began to grin. He began to snigger. He began to chortle. As he slowed his pace at last, he threw back his head and roared with laughter! What fun that was! He pictured the Big People reaching the shed just as he fled, striking the night air with their fists as they saw the wheel barrow and missing clapper! So much for their plan to catch the bogler in the night! Hah! He retraced his steps back home feeling wild and wicked. It was so good to get one up on the Big People!

"Gooshty painterig foor Thom's boot. Seedlies foor Hildi!" Hairy Bogley smacked his lips. "En biggy festli foor meer!" Hildi's cooking was Hairy Bogley's favourite, rarely eaten but never forgotten.

So it was in this happy frame of mind that he reached the rocky steps to his home-cave. The steady rain which fell on to his red hood did not dampen his spirits.

His own home. Away from it all.

Just his.

His alone.

Setting down Herbie Poshtig, tin of paint and roll of wire, Hairy clapped his hands with delight at being there. The noise echoed from the back wall.

And then he froze…

…because in the shadows, something moved.

Disturbed.

Hairy felt the whiskers on the back of his neck prickle and his eyes widened.

Surely not…

Not in *his* cave…

The Something sat up and stretched. A hoarse, rasping cough sounded.

Hairy held his breath. His heart began to thud.

Who was there?

In his home?

~~~

Chapter Four

airy Bogley could stand it no longer. With a sudden rush of panic, he made a lunge to grab Herbie Poshtig, dashed out of the cave and beat a hasty retreat down the mountain path. His breath, held in for so long, now burst from him in great gasps as he took wobbly, knee-knocking leaps from rock to rock in order to escape. Wild thoughts crowded his mind.

Who or what was it?

Why was it there?

He remembered the deep-throated cough that had sounded. It must be an animal, perhaps a wolf or a wolverine. They liked dry caves, he knew, out of this fur-sogging rain. It might be a lynx come down from the North for warmth. Or maybe it was a brown bear, looking for shelter for its cubs, or to find somewhere to lie dormant for the coming winter.

Then with a wave of sickness, another thought occurred to him.

Or a person.

He swallowed, anxiously.

What if it was a Big Person, waiting, ready to pounce on him? To kidnap him and keep him against his will?

Hide.

He must hide.

With relief, Hairy saw a large, craggy boulder a little way ahead of him. In a few troll strides, he reached it and sank to his knees, panting. He glanced at the sky. The rain had stopped and the sky looked clearer. Dawn was not far off. He would wait here for daylight and then creep back to investigate. Perhaps his cave would be empty by then.

Perhaps the Something would have gone.

Perhaps he didn't see or hear anything at all and he had just spooked himself.

As Hairy waited for the pink glimmer of the sun to kiss the fjord water below, he began to feel calmer. He had had a shock, that was all. He knew he was good at bogling so he would be able to approach his cave silently and work out what to do from there. If necessary, he would get the better of his unwelcome guest. In fact, he decided, it could all be rather exciting.

"Yo, yo," he whispered to himself. "Hoo-hoo-hoo!"

~~~

Thom was delighted but puzzled to find the paintbrush on his doorstep when he went to get water the next morning. He brought it to show Hildi who was busily brewing nettle tea to have with a breakfast of fire-roasted mushrooms.

"Looki, Hildi!" he exclaimed as he burst through the door. "Gooshty brushoori foor Mistig Vorter! Strangeror visitori leftig oos brushoori!"

Hildi looked up from her steaming pot and smiled at Thom's enthusiasm. His bright eyes were shining and he wore a broad grin on his walnut face.

"Verisht gooshty, Thom," she replied. She didn't like to point out that he would also need paint to go with the brush if he were to give Mistig Vorter the new coat of blue he wanted. Maybe paint would mysteriously appear also!

The mice had woken up. Tailo's belly started to make rumbling noises that Scratchen could ignore no longer.

"Why don't you jump down from the dresser and find some fallen crumbs to eat, Greedy?" Scratchen suggested. "In fact, come to think of it, there may just be some next to That Cat – just by his right paw!"

For a moment, Tailo looked down in excitement, scrabbling to his feet.

"Where? Where?"

Then he stopped and sighed.

"Gotcha!" snorted Scratchen.

~~~

The time had come. Hairy Bogley slung Herbie Poshtig over his shoulder and cautiously made his way back to his cave. He felt much braver now that he had snoozed for a while, crumpled face up against the rock. Keeping his eyes and ears alert, he crept back home and hid at the side of the entrance.

All seemed quiet. All seemed well.

Hairy ventured out and peered into his home. A waft of smoke met his damp nostrils as he sniffed. Had someone lit a fire in his cave? It definitely couldn't be an animal, then. Curious, Hairy took a step inside.

There was a sudden splutter, followed by a rough cough. Then -

"Onkli Bogley!"

Hairy Bogley blinked twice. There, crouching by a smouldering fire was little Ulf, come to stay with his uncle.

~~~

It was just as Hildi had set down the two steaming mugs of nettle tea and Thom had put the first roast mushroom into his mouth, that Hairy

Bogley burst in through their door, Ulf at his heels. The two trolls, Tracker and Grimo jumped up in alarm.

"Looki!" Hairy shouted, waving his arms madly about him. "Looki - Ulf! Littelor Ulf!" and he pushed Ulf forward with such force that the young troll fell to his little hairy knees on the kitchen floor. Hildi's hands flew to her face and Thom whooped in delight. Grimo took one look and shot out through the open door. Strange, small troll-thing! No thanks!

It had been a long time since Hildi and Thom had seen Ulf. He had been a mere troddler when they last were with him and he had been living on the other side of the fjord. Nobody knew who his mother-troll was and the Other-Side trolls had taken turns to look after him. Now it seemed that it was their turn to house him and so he had made his way to his Uncle Bogley's cave in the hopes that he could stay. All adult trolls were aunties and uncles to the little ones, unless they had mothers and fathers to care for them.

"Ulf, mi littelor dearig!" exclaimed Hildi, picking the young troll up and dusting his knees. "Sitli en eatig brekenfasht. Comli, comli!" and she popped him on a chair at the table with a bowl of tasty mushrooms. Thom motioned to Hairy to take his place and he found another chair for himself. As always, visitors were welcome in the gentle trolls' home.

...and she popped him on a chair

"Who on earth is this little blighter?" squawked Tailo, irritated at the sudden rush of noise when he was expecting a peaceful meal. Scratchen looked down at the gathering from his bed on the dresser and listened carefully to the conversation.

"It seems that this small Ulf visitor has come to stay with Whisker-Face in his smelly cave.

Whisker-Face doesn't sound too chuffed about it actually from what I can gather. You know how he likes to live alone. They are all gabbling stupid troll-talk so quickly it's tricky to work it out."

"All I know is it looks like another two mouths to feed this breakfast, which means less for us starving rodents," grumbled Tailo.

"Whisker-Face is saying that he will let Ulf stay only if he helps him in his work," continued Scratchen, concentrating hard on his translation. "I'm not sure what his work actually is. Hildi and Thom don't seem to know much about it either."

At this point, Hairy Bogley remembered the paint and packet of seeds he had collected for Thom and Hildi. He had left them outside the door and when talk of his work arose, he produced them with a proud flourish.

"Painterig foor Mistig Vorter boot, Thom! En seedlies foor u, Hildi!" he exclaimed. Such was the excitement of the trolls that they all began to talk at once, Thom thanking Hairy and Hildi eagerly examining her gift. Where had he got them from? Did he have to bargain with the Big People? How kind! How thoughtful! How generous!

Tailo wasn't interested in listening any more. He had spotted the fact that the young troll either didn't like mushrooms or he wasn't hungry, because as the older trolls discussed how he could learn collecting skills from his uncle, mushrooms were slipping from his dish on to the floor under his chair. Scratchen was too busy working out the conversation to notice Tailo making his way down the dresser.

Hairy Bogley looked across at his little nephew and sighed. He would have to keep him because no troll should be turned away from the place they had chosen to stay. He reached over and ruffled Ulf's hair. What was more, he was actually beginning to think he could do with a small bogler apprentice to assist him in his collecting. He wiped his mouth on his sleeve, as always, and blew his nose like a trumpet.

"Yo, yo," he agreed at last. "Ulf shtay in Onkli Bogley's homerig."

Hildi looked pleased. It would be good for Hairy to have company and Ulf needed to learn troll skills from an elder. She and Thom could keep an eye on them. It might make Hairy a bit more sociable as well, instead of living his hermit's life. They could visit regularly and perhaps Hairy would learn better habits from Thom. She was concerned about Ulf's cough though. He had coughed and spluttered most of the time they had been talking and he didn't look well.

Hildi scraped back her chair to stand up.

"WHOA!" screeched a familiar voice.

"MY TAIL!"

Everyone looked around them in alarm.

"TAIL – CHAIR LEG! CHAIR LEG – TAIL!"

And there was Tailo, trapped by his tail, surrounded by mushrooms which he was still desperately trying to grasp as they rolled away from him, out of reach.

Hildi quickly picked up the chair and saw not only the mouse, holding his throbbing tail and gnashing his yellow teeth, but also the floor littered with mushrooms. She glanced at Ulf who looked crestfallen and embarrassed. Without a word, Hildi scooped up the discarded breakfast bits and threw them out of the kitchen window.

"Hey! WHOA! What?" screeched Tailo at the sight of his treat disappearing. "Those were *mine*!" and forgetting his pinched tail, scrabbled up the wall and jumped out after them.

Ulf swallowed. His big eyes filled as he looked up at Hildi and he coughed once more. He rubbed his little rough hands up and down his arms to warm himself as he started to shiver.

"Ulf nics hungeror, Antoori Hildi," he whispered. "Ulf feelen badli."

Hildi knew exactly what to do. She was adept at making all manner of medicines from the herbs she collected in the forest. It was essential some trolls knew these skills because they couldn't go for help from the Big People, wary of the danger they would put themselves in. She also used Thom's heather honey to help keep cuts clean and heal wounds more quickly. She made wonderful honey cough drops, honey-garlic elixir and honey brandy for winter nights. In no time at all, a bubbling mass was cooking over the fire and Ulf was wrapped up warmly, sitting in front of it.

~~~

Tailo had stuffed himself with mushrooms and, after licking his sore tail and washing his whiskers, decided to scamper through the forest in the search of something sweet to freshen his mouth. His pattering feet scurried over pine needles and fallen cones, up and over broken sticks and branches, through heather and gorse. His eager nose twitched and sniffed, desperate to find the scent of yellow cloudberries or perhaps some blueberries. His ears and eyes were constantly alert, watching for signs of danger. It was not unknown for foxes and badgers to be about – and then there was always the chance That Cat might be strolling by. Tailo didn't intend to become an elevenses snack for him!

Then, all at once, there was a sudden rumbling. The ground began to tremble under the little mouse's paws. He stopped and raised his whiskers, sniffing the air. There was a smoky smell, but not that of cooking or of a bonfire. He looked through a gap in the trees and saw a blue, choking cloud rising into the air. Tailo began to feel alarmed. This was not good in a forest; not good at all.

The rumbling suddenly became a roar and the ground thundered and shook. Grouse and woodcocks shot out from the undergrowth and fled in panic on to the exposed forest path, feathers flapping and flying. The sky above became black with birds as they left their nests in the trees and took to their wings. A reindeer darted out from the shadows, startled and skittish, kicking its back legs in the air – a flash of its white tail and it was gone. Tailo looked around him in desperation. His claws were gripping on to the ground as if any minute it would slip away from him and he would be hurled into a vicious maelstrom of thunderous danger.

"EARTHQUAKE!" he screeched, eyes popping. "CRIPES! HELP ME!" and he raced to a nearby log over which the reindeer had vaulted. It was rotten, but hollow and as such provided some protection. The terrified mouse forced his fat body in at the end and curled up into a tight ball squeezing shut his beady eyes as the ground seemed to take blow after pounding blow.

~~~

Far away in the tranquil home of the trolls, Scratchen stretched in his bed on the dresser. For once he had been able to eat in solitude and he had finished all the scraps piled for both mice. He lazily kick-kicked the fur around his neck and scritchscratched his tummy. He wondered where his little matey had got to. His only concern was that Grimo had also gone outside and you never could tell with That Cat. It was more than likely that Tailo had found a wonderful pile of nut clusters though and was scoffing them right now so that he didn't have to share them, he thought. He was bound to be absolutely fine and appear all smug before long. No need to worry.

The black mouse nevertheless kept one eye open, watching the window for the familiar round ball of brown fur, of whom he was ridiculously fond.

It was when the cuckoo clock told Scratchen of the passing of time that he really began to wonder. Hildi was fussing over Ulf who was looking decidedly perkier and Thom had disappeared with shuffling Hairy Bogley to store his precious paint inside Mistig Vorter. Neither Grimo nor Tailo had returned for several hours and this was very unusual. He decided he must investigate. Tracker would have to help. With his nose and Scratchen's bright eyes, they were bound to find cat, or mouse.

And so it was that a little black mouse, clinging valiantly on to the scruff of a sniffing dog's neck, came across a sight not seen before in the forest.

Fallen trees were lined up in a row, one after the other, their branches splintered and broken. Cones and needles lay scattered, cruelly discarded.

A huge saw lay on the ground, its teeth surrounded by sawdust and shavings. Biting chains bound the pines tightly ready to drag them from their place of birth, growth and splendour.

And then…

The dog suddenly whined and dropped to the ground. Memories of cruelty and bullying flooded his mind.

Harsh words.

Rough voices.

Kicking boots and whipping sticks.

Tracker flattened himself to the forest floor shutting his eyes to control his fear. Scratchen cowered in the ruff of fur. His mousey teeth began to chatter as he trembled.

For through the clearing, they could see quite distinctly a Big Person, sitting on the step to the cab of a huge Dyno-Truk.

~~~

Chapter Five

ight fell quickly. Gathering clouds bunched cheek to cheek, cloaking the sky in thick grey. Bats began to flit through the treetops but found few insects to flick their tongues at in the damp air. Ulf followed, a few troll-steps behind his Uncle's hairy feet, towards the peeping lights below. He was feeling much better as a result of Hildi's loving care, although his tickly cough still worried away at his throat, scratching like a tiny, stuck ant. He was nervous, but excited and most definitely up for an adventure.

Hairy Bogley had wondered if tonight was the best time to introduce Ulf to his first lesson in bogling, but being at a loss as to what else to do with his young visitor, he had packed some of Hildi's medicine in Herbie Poshtig and made for the town. What *did* you do with young trolls these days? Hairy couldn't even remember how it felt to be so little. He had nothing to feed Ulf with and hadn't liked to admit this to Hildi, who would have been shocked. Hairy just didn't do the food, cooking thing if he could help it. Perhaps they would be able to find some bread for breakfast and a piece of cake. Something simple to start off with, then.

"Onkli Bogley?" Ulf called out as if reading Hairy's thoughts. "Ulf feelen hungeror, Onkli!"

"Shh!"

Ulf shrugged his shoulders and skipped on. He stood on the tip of his troll toes to see further down the path.

"Onkli Bogley?" Ulf called out once more. "Ulf feelen dursty, Onkli!"

"Shh! Shh!"

Ulf fell silent and continued to follow. The lights below were much closer now and Hairy Bogley slowed his pace, waiting. Silently, he peered through the trees, watching out for Big People.

Ulf felt a tickle in his throat. He swallowed and rubbed his neck with a tiny hand. It tickled again - and a cough burst out in a sudden bark.

"Dunder-troll, Ulf! Shh! Shh! Shh!"

This bogler-training was not going to be easy.

~~~

Like the other animals, Grimo had also come across the savagery in the forest. He too had seen the once majestic trees snared and captured, trussed up to be disposed of. He too had been horrified to find a Big Person in their woodland. He too had dashed for cover when the deafening roar of the Dyno-Truk had started up and, with a smoking screech of engine and tyres, had bludgeoned its way down the forest path to the town.

The engine smoke hung in the air smothering the fragrance of pine and all became completely still.

New deep ruts were left in the ground alongside the slaughtered pines.

Grimo let out an enormous howl in the emptiness.

He h-o-w-l-e-d and he h-o-w-l-e-d and he h-o-w-l-e-d.

Terrified, Tracker opened his eyes wide. Another family member out here, frantic in the forest! Grimo! Scratchen sat up straight on the dog's back. His eyes searched for a sign of the cat. Love him or hate him, they must stick together for protection and get home fast.

Somewhere deep inside a hollow log, a shaking fat brown ball of fur began to uncurl. Tailo had heard Grimo too and knew that this was his only chance. He did not understand what had been happening at all. He just knew that if he could return to his bed on the warm dresser he would never leave home again! His only hope was to trust the mouse-basher.

"Hey – CAT!" he screeched from inside his log. "Over HEE-YER!" His squeaky voice was magnified and boomed out of the end, echoing through the wood.

Hee-yer! Hee-yer! Hee-yer!

Grimo's howling ceased in time to hear the last sound of the echoing cry and he located Tailo in a flash. Tracker sniffed the air and, making nothing of it except engine fumes, put nose to ground and soon picked up the cat's scent. Within minutes the four animals were together - mice wary of cat, cat wary of dog - but together, and ready for home, where Hildi and Thom were waiting, anxiously.

~~~

Topped up with cough medicine once more, Hairy Bogley's admonishments still ringing in his ears, Ulf was doing his best to bogle along the road. His earlier skipping had been fine along the forest path but now they were in Big People territory and great care was needed. He concentrated hard, studying his whiskery Uncle's gait and the way he placed his flat feet swiftly but silently on the ground. With fists clenched and elbows moving like duck wings, Ulf imitated the bogle as best he could until Hairy Bogley stopped and crouched behind a bush.

In front of them was a small shack of a house. Its windows were dingy and without curtains or lights. The front door was tatty and not hung straight in its frame. Bins, overflowing with boxes and papers and bottles and peelings, were stacked in the corner against a broken-down wall. A black Dyno-Truk was parked outside.

A black Dyno-Truk with forest mud on its tyres.

Hairy Bogley had been here before. He remembered the delicious hen's leg he had found discarded in one of the bins and the piece of claggy cake left in a lunch box on the seat of the Truk. He smiled as he remembered his cave dance that night, with keys jangling from his ear. Perhaps they could get another set tonight to make a matching pair!

Ulf appeared at his side and tugged at Hairy's trouser leg.

"Onkli?"

"Shh!"

"Ulf bogle Biggy Menor's homerig, Onkli?"

"Shh! Shh!"

"Onkli? Es excitig, Onkli!"

"Shh! Shh! Shh!"

And Hairy clapped a grimy hand over the little troll's mouth as he bent down low to whisper, "Ulf musten shh! Liker littelor morsi!"

Ulf tried his best to squeak-eek like a mouse but his Uncle's grip was too firm.

~~~

Hildi and Thom flung open the door to their dwelling at the first sound of their dear ones on the path outside. Their pets bounded across the threshold with howls, wuffs, squeaks and screeches, each desperately trying to get best position nearest the cosy fire and away from the door.

"Mi lovelor dearigs! Doggor! Pussor! Morsies!" cried Hildi in dismay and gathered them together in her arms.

Thom secured the door against the night's damp and joined them. His brow was furrowed and his weathered face was full of concern. Something serious must have happened for the animals to be so upset.

Little by little, the four calmed themselves and began to work together to explain what they had witnessed in the forest. The two trolls looked on in bewilderment.

Grimo nudged at the basket of firewood in the hearth and between them, mice and cat stood three small pieces of kindling up on end to represent trees in the forest. Tracker then cowered down low in front of them and growled, whilst Scratchen jumped on to the back of his neck and Tailo scampered around looking for cover. When he was safely inside an old plant pot, Grimo, with tail fuzzed and back arched trying to look his fiercest, stood up on back legs and, balancing carefully, approached the kindling. It wasn't at all easy – how did these Big People and trolls walk like this? Sure that all was in position and that he had the full attention of everyone, Grimo took a massive swipe at the little tree models and with a clatter they fell into the hearth, scattering ash and wood chippings. Tracker put his paws over his ears and Grimo charged around the room looking for shelter under the table.

Thom and Hildi were astounded. What could it all mean? They had never seen their animals so agitated before and, without doubt, they were trying to tell them something important.

"Dearigs," Thom began, beckoning them to his side as he sat next to the fire. "Dedden in foresh, yo?"

The pets nodded vigorously.

"Biggy Menor in foresh?" asked Hildi remembering Tracker's cowering and growling.

Tracker whined as he nodded his great head, looking at the trolls with sad eyes. Thom ruffled the fur on the dog's head and scruffled him under the chin. He knew about Tracker's past and what this would mean to him. He thought about the tumbling firewood Grimo had so spectacularly crashed over, balancing on his hind legs, looking fierce and menacing.

"Wooden choppen? Biggy wooden choppen? Biggy Menor wooden choppen?" he questioned gently.

All the animals howled, wuffed and squeaked at once. Thom was beginning to get the picture.

"Thom choppen urnli littelor wooden foor fior – nics biggy wooden."

He could see now why the animals were so distraught. Big People must be chopping down trees in the forest. He had heard about this. They would be clearing whole areas.

This was bad news.

This meant the forest could change.

This was dangerous for animals, plants - and trolls.

~~~

Ulf understood his instructions. He had listened carefully and tried very hard not to interrupt too much in his excitement. There was a window which was not quite closed. It wasn't big enough for a full grown troll to climb through... but a little one...perhaps...

Once inside, Ulf was to look for something tasty to eat and bring it out to Hairy Bogley. He didn't stop for a minute to question whether this was a good way to behave. He didn't stop for a minute to question whether this was the sort of thing a young impressionable troll like himself should be learning. He didn't stop for a minute to ask himself whether it was risky or dangerous or indeed sensible. All Ulf knew was that his Uncle had told him to do it. He wanted to show Hairy Bogley that he could be a good bogler and it was worth taking him on as an apprentice and giving him a good home in recognition of this.

Hairy, it must be said, did have some misgivings. He thought briefly of his responsibility in bringing up Ulf and how Hildi and Thom would react if they knew he wasn't tucked up in a warm blanket in front of a fire for the night. Especially with that cough. Also, he wasn't at all sure that Ulf was the right troll for the job. This bothered him the most. It didn't occur to him that what he was doing was wrong. Big People obviously left things for him to find because they were careless or didn't need them any more.

Simple as that.

That's what he told himself anyway.

With a silent nod of his head, Hairy Bogley gave the trainee bogler a leg-up to the window and then hid in the bushes to wait, grimy fingers crossed.

Ulf scrabbled at the window ledge and managed to cling on, little fluffy legs dangling. He looked to the left and to the right.

"Oh dearig," he thought. "Onkli?" he whispered into the shadows. "Onkli Bogley?"

"Shh!" Hairy Bogley waved him on with an impatient gesture.

Ulf had to be brave. He had to prove himself. He stretched out a trembling hand and gently pushed the window. It opened further and a warm fug of stale air escaped, catching his breath. He stifled a cough, forcing his throat to clamp it down. Mustn't cough now! Hooking a foot over the window ledge, he climbed inside and dropped to the floor.

As he peered into the gloom, he could see the shapes of boots, huge boots, Big People's huge boots, abandoned in the doorway. Kicked off and muddied. A discarded coat lay where it was thrown on the floor. A drip-drip-dripping tap drip-drip-dripped into an old chipped sink. Ulf blinked in time to the drips and then, with a dry mouth, sweaty hands and a thumping heart, began to search.

~~~

Hildi and Thom had settled their dear ones at last. The mice had been fed with dry herb bread and lovingly placed on their safe dresser to sleep off their worries. Grimo had been given smoked fish bits and had found an old firewood box to curl up in. He had licked himself so clean that he glistened in the firelight. Then his eyes had glazed over and he

78

snuggled his smoky-grey nose into his soft tummy fur, snoring gently. Tracker, as usual, lay at Thom's troll feet, great head on outstretched paws.

Hildi's cheeks were two cherry red patches of anxiety. In urgent whispers, so as not to disturb their animals, the two trolls discussed the future of the forest. They both knew it was not just the loss of trees that was at stake.

"Vildi floweries, nay morish!" murmured Hildi.

"Nay bilbooren en mushroomer!" muttered Thom.

"Nay morish herbies!" Hildi thought of her medicines and scented sprays to hang from rafters.

The trolls shook their heads. Without trees, the life of everything they loved and relied upon would be threatened. All the plants which thrived in woodland would be affected. Shade-loving plants would be exposed to light and winds. The ground would be laid bare. Mushroom collecting would be more difficult; bilberry bushes would be cleared. Wild flowers would disappear as roads and paths were made for trucks to travel along. Heathers for Thom's honey bees would be destroyed.

Hildi had a sudden thought. Her hand flew to her mouth as she took an intake of breath.

"Thom! Animores!" Her eyes filled. "Littleor animores, Thom!"

Thom knelt beside Hildi and took her fragile hands, wet with tears in his strong, capable grasp. They thought of all the small forest animals from the tiniest tree beetle to the snuffling hedgehog, rooting for worms. They thought of the forest mice, foxes, rabbits and hares. They thought of all the creepies and the crawlies who worked so hard to play their part in the everyday workings of forest life. All without trees and hidey-holes to live in.

"En biggy animores!" Thom whispered grimly.

What he said was true. Larger animals also relied upon the forest for food and shelter. From the shy badgers to the few reindeer who loved to strip bark, to the howling wolverines and shuffling bears.

And the birds. The night owls.

Where would they build their nests? Their precious homes...

Then sudden realisation struck Thom, which sent a wave of sickness washing over him.

The trolls themselves could be discovered.

~~~

Ulf's throat tickled. In the darkness of the Truk driver's house, he rubbed at his neck and swallowed. Best get out as quickly as possible, before he had to cough. He moved as quietly as he could, searching for something of interest. Anything that might please his Uncle. He stretched out his arms in front of him, groping around the room.

A shuffle here, a bogle there.
A tickle in his throat.
Looking up, looking down, looking all around.
A tickle in his throat.
In this cupboard, in that drawer.

A tickle in his throat.

Then –

THWACK!

A sudden sharp pain thudded into Ulf's knee as he banged into a table leg, making him wince. The little troll held his breath to stop his cough and bit his lip. He trembled as he heard the bark of a disturbed dog and voices from upstairs.

"Did you lock up properly, Ogmund?"

"Yes, yes, of course!"

There was a brief pause.

"Ogmund? Did you hear the dog bark? Is he all right?"

"Yes, yes, of course!"

Another pause.

"So everything *is* secure?"

"Yes, yes, of course!"

Silence.

Ulf tiptoed across the floor. He had to be quick now. He didn't want to be in that house a moment longer than he had to be. There was a sort of a cupboard with a white curved door in front of him. It looked promising. It was different from the other cupboards which were dark wood and disappointingly contained only pots and boxes. He stretched out a tiny troll arm and pulled at the handle.

Whoooosh!

A shaft of bright light flooded over him and a rush of freezing cold air hit him smack in the face.

Startled and gasping, the little tickle Ulf had in his throat suddenly exploded!

In seconds, the door of the room had swung open with a tremendous *BANG!* and Ulf found himself swinging high in the air, held by the belt of his little blue trousers.

~~~

Chapter Six

hom! Hildi! Hildi! Thom!" The peace of the trolls' home was shattered by a great clattering and clamouring as Hairy Bogley, whiskers flying wildly and eyes popping, pelted up the path.

"Littelor Ulf! Biggy Menor! Dedden Biggy Menor hab littlelor Ulf!"

Thom leapt out of bed leaving Hildi shaking, patchwork quilt pulled up around her quaking chin with trembling fingers. Whatever could have happened? What on earth was all the noise about? The door slammed open, shuddering in its crooked wooden frame, as Hairy burst in.

"Badli Biggy Menor! Nay! Nay! Dedden! Dedden!" shouted Hairy, dashing around the little kitchen table in a frenzy.

"EARTHQUAKE! EARTHQUAKE!" Tailo screeched for the second time in as many days, clinging valiantly on to the edge of the dresser as it rocked precariously. "HELP! HELP!"

Grimo dived for cover under the quilt next to Hildi's hairy feet and Tracker sprang on to the bed, covering his head with Thom's downy pillow.

"Bogley!" Thom cried out, trying to control wild troll dashings and yet hold the dresser still at the same time. "Bogley – shtop! Pleasor shtop!"

"Badli Menor!" Hairy shouted in anguish. "Badli Biggy Menor hab Ulf!" and he sank in a heap of apologies and babble on Hildi and Thom's floor.

Little by little, the two trolls managed to get the story from him. They were shocked to hear that Hairy Bogley had taken little Ulf out for the night to visit houses of Big People. Hildi thought of the young troll; how he had coughed and felt ill, the medicine she had given him to help, thinking all the while that Hairy would look after him. Even so, she couldn't be cross with Hairy as he was absolutely inconsolable and Thom had to give him some Troll-Cherry Wine to calm his nerves. What Thom said was true: the important thing was to find Ulf and bring him home.

Tailo and Scratchen were not at all impressed. They had endured enough trauma in the forest and the one safe, calm place in their lives was supposed to be their bed on the dresser. When they realised what all the fuss was about, both turned tail on the troll gathering and scampered into a corner where they proceeded to gnaw at the wood in protest. Their aim was to chew their way into the cupboard next to the dresser where Hildi kept all manner of tasty snacks. Would serve them right, the mice thought, in full agreement for once. Waking them up like that! Making all this fuss over that odd little troll person! Forgetting their breakfast!

Together the three trolls discussed the situation. Whilst Hildi and Thom didn't understand Hairy Bogley's work or behaviour, neither of them thought it helpful to scold him. What did it matter what his reasons were? They had to find Ulf!

This, however, was The Problem.

Hairy could not describe how to find his nephew. The paths he bogled along were so well known to him that he went down them without thinking, and took so many twists and turns that it was impossible to describe where he went. He was also in no fit state to take them there. They did not know what they would face, if and when they found Ulf, and Hairy Bogley being wild and hysterical would not help.

Tracker had come out from under the pillow by now to rest at Thom's feet, listening to the conversation. He knew he could help. He looked up at his master and whined, scraping gentle paws on Thom's knee.

"Tracker?" Thom questioned. "Tracker helpen oos? Hor?"

At this, the dog put his nose to the floor and searched for Ulf's scent. Under the table, he located the chair which had held the little troll's dangling legs and from there he followed the trail to the door where he had left with his uncle the previous day. In a flash, Thom was beside him, tucking his troll tail into his green dungarees and blowing Hildi a kiss.

"Nay worrish, Hildi!" he called reassuringly. "Tracker findor Ulf en fetchen homerig! Gooshty borg – kissig, kissig!"

With a wave of his hand, Thom ran after the dog who was already halfway down their path.

…gentle paws on Thom's knee…

~~~

Ulf shuffled uncomfortably in his confined space. He was locked in a small cupboard, the only light coming through the keyhole and the only air from where it fitted so badly in its frame. He was worn out and utterly miserable. It had been a long night, cramped as he was, and he longed to stretch his little furry legs.

Oh why had he coughed so loudly?

What was he going to do?

"Oh, Onkli Bogley," he sighed as hot tears began to run down his crumpled face. "Ulf feelen so sadli, Onkli Bogley."

Voices came to his ears. The voices of the Big People. He snatched back his sobs to listen.

"Little squirt!" a woman was saying. "Coming into my house in the dead of night, rooting through my cupboards, pinching my stuff! How dare he? I hope you're going to do something about him!"

"Yes, yes, of course!" came the reply.

"Little sneak-thief!" snorted the woman. "I bet you anything he was the one who came here before and stole your Truk keys! Where would you have been without your spares? If you couldn't drive your Truk, you couldn't work and your work is vital to us."

"Yes, yes, of course!"

"Little burglar! I think he should be made to pay! Have you thought about that?"

"Yes, yes, of course!"

Ulf strained to hear every word he could. He had to keep sniffing because his nose was running so much and he couldn't reach a tiny hanky that Hildi had given him. The thought of her kindness made him even more upset and he began to cry again.

"Little sniveller! Can you hear him?" The woman's voice was sharp and cruel. "I think you should make him work for you – a kind of Community Service for all the trouble he's caused! Are you listening, Ogmund?"

"Yes, yes, of course!"

~~~

As the woodland path before them twisted downwards to the town, Thom felt his first nagging doubt. Certainly Tracker was on the right trail, for his pace never faltered and his nose did not lift from the ground. The dog would, without doubt, eventually bring him to Ulf and Thom knew the young troll needed his help.

But where would this trail lead to?

What would he find?

What would he do?

~~~

Tailo whooped in mouse delight! He had made a breakthrough and, although his yellow teeth felt a bit wobbly and his jaw ached with the effort, his twitching nose-end told him a route into the next door cupboard was his at last. Scratchen clapped his paws together, had a quick kick-kick round his neck, and joined his Partner-in-Crime. The hole was only tiny but it was enough to allow delicious smells of dry biscuits, bread and cheese to escape. The two mice breathed in deeply. The fat brown mouse drew himself up importantly.

"Your mission," announced Tailo grandly, "should you wish to accept it..." He paused for maximum effect and to ensure Scratchen was suitably impressed. "...is to develop this breakthrough hole in a Secretive Manner…Indeed, yours is to be a Secret Mission…"

Scratchen raised one mousey eyebrow.

"Using wile and cunning and determination."

("Where do I get 'wile' from?" wondered Scratchen, confused.)

"Against all odds, you will succeed, gnawing and working with dedication, to enhance this breakthrough hole so easier access can be gained…"

Again Tailo paused.

Scratchen waited.

Tailo lowered his voice and glanced from left to right.

"…to The Other Side!"

Tailo finished his little speech with a flourish of his paw, pointing through the tiny hole. In so doing, he lost balance and fell flat on his round bottom, losing a certain amount of dignity.

Scratchen sighed and lazily kick-kicked to show he was not impressed by the other mouse's grandeur.

"So what you're saying is that you want me to chew away at this wood, to make your tiny hole into the cupboard next door big enough for you to fit your fat belly through. Am I right?"

"Well," replied Tailo, looking a little annoyed, "in a manner of speaking, yes!" He glared at Scratchen now. "Yes! Yes! Get on with it! Now!"

"Haven't you forgotten something?" asked Scratchen, nonchalantly inspecting the tip of his black tail.

"No," replied the other mouse. "I have worked out a magnificent plan and given you clear instructions. I want you to - "

Scratchen tutted, putting his tail down.

"Oh *really*? You *want* me to ..." He stopped to fix Tailo with a hard stare. "What's the little word?"

Tailo looked shame-faced. He wriggled and shuffled awkwardly as if the word would choke him.

"Well?" demanded Scratchen.

A pause.

More wriggling and shuffling.

"I said, 'Well?'"

"Please?"

~~~

Thom whistled to Tracker to make him stop. They were approaching the outskirts of the town and the bright daylight would provide no cover. In his haste to leave, he had not thought of any disguise or how to conceal his troll-ness. His tail, he knew would be a real give-away and had been tucked into the back of his dungarees, but Thom wore no shirt or shoes and, compared with Big People, he was pretty hairy. He looked around him but saw nothing that would be of any use. He would just have to approach with great caution and not be seen by anyone.

Tracker whined and took a few steps along the path to where the paving of the road began. He was keen to find Ulf and didn't want to waste time.

"Dedden, Tracker!" Thom warned. "Biggy Menor catchen Ulf. Nics catchen Thom!"

Tracker understood. He gave Thom a great slobbery lick and went on ahead, alone. Thom crept into a nearby bush and peered out through the scratchy branches to watch his dog disappear down the road.

~~~

Hildi had warmed some soothing honey-water and, with reassuring tones, had calmed Hairy Bogley down. They sat together in the little wooden kitchen with the fire smoking gently and watched the hands on the cuckoo clock. They seemed to move so slowly! When would they get some news?

Grimo, deciding that all was quiet once more, slipped out from the patchwork quilt and stretched his paws out in front of him, admiring his recently sharpened claws. Plan for today? He wasn't sure he had thought of one yet. As he began to consider, one smoky-grey ear twitched backwards and his amber eyes widened.

Exactly *what* were those mice up to?

~~~

The sudden light made Ulf blink and draw his hand over his eyes as his prison cupboard door was unlatched and he was pulled roughly from his cramped position by his ear.

"So, little troll," sneered Birna, "the time has come for you to earn your keep!" She thrust her grisly face close to his so that he could see grey beardy bits growing on her chin and smell her fetid breath. "You have broken into our house with evil in mind and now you have been caught!"

"Im nics badli!" Ulf protested indignantly, finding his voice at last. "Im gooshty Ulf!"

"Have you heard the squawking, Ogmund?" the woman shouted out to her husband. "He sounds like a trapped pig! What a little coward!" Dragging Ulf into another room she began to laugh cruelly. "Here he is! Our troll-servant. At your service!" and Birna flung Ulf to where Ogmund sat. He crouched down low in a sorry little heap.

Ogmund nudged the troll with one huge foot. It was covered in dirty grey sock holes and a cheesy-smelling toe jabbed at Ulf making him look up.

Nothing was said.

Ulf felt sick. The menacing smile on this Big Person's face wasn't at all welcoming. He clasped his hands together pleadingly and dared to look into the hard black eyes which studied him.

"Pleasor!" Ulf begged. "Ulf nics shtay in strangeror homerig. Pleasor!"

"Pah!" spat the woman baring her large, yellow teeth. "Have you heard him whining now? First he squawks, then he whines. What a thoroughly miserable specimen he is!" Birna reached out and gave Ulf a hard pinch. "No meat on you either – you're going to have to toughen up if you are going to work for my Ogmund!"

Ulf drew his furry knees up to his chest as he crouched on the floor beneath the man's feet.

Work? For them? Servant? How?

"Tell him then, Ogmund! About the forest. About tree-felling and rope–tying and branch-cutting and sawing! About clearing the area for roads and houses and shops! About how rich it's going to make us! And how hard he's going to work for you!"

The man cleared his throat and got to his feet.

"Yes, yes, of course!"

He yanked Ulf up and the little troll hung his head, great fat tears plopping on to his furry feet.

~~~

The mice were in!

Scratchen had broken through first and he had managed to tug and pull and pull and tug Tailo through the hole which led to The Other Side. He had burst in like a cork from a bottle and had fallen amongst oat biscuits and rye bread. He was in Paradise!

"Oh yes!" he squealed in ecstasy. "Get stuck in, Scratchen!" and he abandoned himself to frantic gobbling, barely swallowing before stuffing more into his mouth.

Grimo flicked his tail.

"Mmm, yum, yum! Thiff if fo gub!" Tailo gruffled into his food, unable to get his words out clearly.

"Weren't you ever told not to talk with your mouth stuffed?" questioned Scratchen tartly, daintily nibbling at a crust.

"Nope!"

Grimo slunk to the base of the cupboard. He flicked his tail again.

"Weren't you ever told not to be greedy?"

"Never!" declared Tailo. "In fact, it is with some pride that I can say I have always been congratulated on my ability to eat vast quantities in a short space of time!"

Pride, of course, always comes before a fall. Just as Hildi walked over to get an oatmeal biscuit for Hairy Bogley, Grimo saw his chance. Unable to contain himself a moment longer, he launched pell-mell into the opened cupboard. He plunged at Tailo, ears back and pink mouth gaping. Tailo screeched and leap-frogged over Scratchen who jumped nimbly from shelf to shelf, cascading oats and breadcrusts down to Hildi's feet.

"Nay, nay, animores! Shoo! Shoo!" she yelled. "Badli animores! Verisht badli!"

As if things weren't bad enough for her! In a rare show of irritation, Hildi reached for her twiggy broom and all were swept out of the door. Hairy Bogley looked pleased. All the biscuits were broken and scattered on the floor. It looked just like his home-cave!

~~~

Tracker had heard enough. He had located Ulf without difficulty and listened, ears cocked, to the sound of the Big People discussing his future. Now he raced back to Thom, breathless and panting, pulling and tugging at his dungarees, desperate to take him to the house. Thom had seen Tracker flying up the road towards him and knew he had to act. This dog was distressed.

So, forgetting all caution, they returned. Just in time to see Ulf being bundled into the Dyno-Truk, eyes wide and terrified, as it roared towards the forest in a cloud of choking smoke.

~~~

Chapter Seven

ithout doubt, something had to be done. Tracker and Thom had come home with heavy hearts and a feeling of sick dread. Many hours had been spent, long into the night, discussing Ulf's plight. To rescue him would be dangerous and difficult. To leave him with the Big People was unthinkable. They considered approaching Ogmund and Birna to ask for him back, but shuddered at the thought of becoming captives themselves. They wondered if they could ask for help from other Big People, but who would they ask? Who could they trust?

Hairy Bogley even considered plundering some of the Troll Treasure from the cavern hidden deep underground, behind the Great Waterfall. Surely the Big People would want to do a deal with them over that! Great wealth was supposed to be hidden there by Troll forefathers, to be used in times of dire need.

But, no.

Hairy knew, like Thom and Hildi, that the Troll Treasure should be protected at all costs, with their lives if necessary. It belonged to all trolls. It was not to be squandered or thought of lightly. It could not be used to save just one unfortunate troll, however desperate. The Troll Treasure was for all trolls throughout the land.

With drooping tails and sagging shoulders, Hairy lowering himself to the floor by the dimming fire, all finally resigned themselves to a sleepless night, wondering what the next day might bring.

~~~

A scout bee had taken a wrong turn. It had left the swarm and was searching for a new home for part of the colony. It flew in through the open kitchen window which Grimo used as a cat flap and settled buzzily on the end of the little wooden bed. This wasn't going to be right at all. It needed a dry, *dark* shelter, perhaps in an attic or tree hollow, which was big enough for the swarm to set up happy honey-making. This sunshine bright bedroom with flapping red and white checked curtains just would not do. It buzzed in annoyance and sat rubbing its legs over its golden body.

Tracker raised an ear. Was that a bee-buzz?

The scout took to the air and began to zoom into all corners of the room, up against the wooden beams and down on to the neatly-swept floor. No way out. It settled once more to consider. It had to get back to the swarm soon. They were nesting just outside Thom's hives and were restless to move on. The queen was getting older and had demanded a new home, as their old one was becoming cramped at the end of the season's nectar collection.

Another bee-buzz and another zoom.

Tracker was sure now. Wary as he was of burning stings, he still had a home to protect!

With a growl, he snapped at the bee as it dipped and dived, zooming faster and faster around the room leaving his cross head spinning.

The bee landing on snoring Hairy Bogley's nose was a definite mistake though. With a great bear-like grunt, Hairy took a deep breath and sucked it into his gaping mouth right back to his tonsils. The sudden onslaught of manic buzz-buzzing made him splutter awake, gagging, coughing and choking. The soggy bee with wet, limp wings was spat out just as Tracker bounded across the floor to protect the visitor and thudded on top of Hairy's chest.

"Stoofid dunder doggor!" yelled Hairy Bogley when he could breathe again. "SHTOP Tracker, SHTOP!"

First a choking, then this pounding; not the best way to wake up at all!

"NAY, NAY, Hairy Bogley!" shouted Thom leaping out of bed. "Tracker comli meer! Gooshty doggor!"

The scout bee scowled at them all. Fresh air from the kitchen window wafted in its direction, drying its wings and showing the escape route. They just weren't worth the sting.

Thom looked at the buzzer thoughtfully as it disappeared into the morning freshness. He knew all about bees. He knew his hives were full. He knew his queen was restless.

"Hmm," he wondered.

~~~

Before any plan to rescue Ulf could take shape properly, it was decided that some reconnaissance work was needed. With this in mind, feeling calmer now they were doing something positive, Thom and Hairy Bogley set off on a fact-finding mission. Hildi had lovingly packed wedges of rye bread and a small pot of honey into her Herbie Poshtig, together with a bottle of best nettle cordial, well-known to soothe in stressful moments, and it was not long before the two intrepid trolls found fresh tracks of the Dyno-Truk carved into the forest path.

As they travelled, the path widened and it became clear that trees were missing. In the distance they could see a faint plume of smoke. The rough, grating sound of an engine came to their ears. Thom whispered an unnecessary word of warning to Hairy Bogley (after all, wasn't bogling in silence what he did best?) and they proceeded with caution, keeping eyes and ears alert.

At last they saw him…

…the dejected little figure of Ulf trailing behind the Big Person. Together, they watched as instructions were barked at him and he began to drag logs from where they had been sawn, to the Truk, ready for loading. He looked exhausted. His tiny troll tuft of a tail drooped miserably and his face was smeared with mud where he had wiped his tears away. Sniffing and coughing badly, Ulf returned time and time again to the pile of severed branches to grapple at them with blistered fingers. The Big Person had toppled tree after tree. Thunderingly, they had crashed to the forest floor where they were chopped, sawn with relentless metal teeth and trussed up.

No animals were to be seen or heard in this part of the forest.

It seemed as if there were no birds in the tree tops.

All gone.

Fled and flown.

As Hairy Bogley and Thom spied from their hide-away place, Ulf's knees buckled under him for the third time. He fell to the ground, grazing his furry legs and little poky elbows. The watching trolls winced in sympathy and cast each other worried frowns.

How much more could Ulf take?

He was so young. So small. So poorly.

Ogmund stopped sawing and wiped his brow. Sweat was trickling down his puffed red face as he glared at his worker, lying face down on the forest floor.

"Get up, little twit!" he sneered. "Can't even take a morning's work! My Birna was right. You *are* going to have to toughen up if you are to be of any use to me!"

Ulf didn't move.

Ogmund grunted and strode over to him. He shoved a great boot at Ulf's side, rolling him over.

"I said: 'GET UP!'" he bawled.

Ulf began to struggle to his feet. It was clear that he ached all over and needed to rest. He crouched down and put his sorry head in his sore hands.

"No use sitting there, my lad! I need my lunch – go fetch it from the Truk!"

Ulf looked up at this. He turned his round, sad eyes upwards and stared at the figure looming above him.

"Pleasor, Ulf feelen hungeror."

Ogmund grabbed Ulf by his spiky hair and hoisted him harshly to his feet. He thrust his cruel, hot face down towards the little troll and laughed out loud.

"No good begging me in that daft language of yours, mate – or any other language for that matter – I aint listening! Now go get my lunch!" and he pushed Ulf towards the Truk as he settled himself on a comfy bank, with his back up against one of the remaining standing trees.

Thom and Hairy Bogley watched with rising indignation and concern as their nephew did as he was told. A large pack of bread and meat was collected from the front seat of the Truk and dutifully

101

placed in the Big Person's lap. Ulf then sat at Ogmund's feet, like a beaten dog, flinching at every harsh word spoken.

"So, worker-troll," Ogmund said through a stuffed mouth, spit running down his chin, "are you enjoying life in the real world?" and he chuckled to himself as he tore some meat from its bone with his tombstone teeth.

Ulf made no reply.

"Have to say, I'm rather glad you did drop in that evening, actually. Was just thinking I needed a lackey! And you're better at fetching and carrying than I thought – except you're rather scrawny!"

Ogmund tossed the bone he had been chewing, up high into the air. It bounced off a distant tree trunk and a last solitary bird called out in panic, finally lost its nerve and flew its nest. The Big Man glanced up at the tree from where the bird had flown and a slow smile broke across his face. He could see, quite plainly, that there was a carefully woven nest swaying gently on the branch. Pausing from his greedy munching for a moment, he stood up, collected a long iron bar from the Dyno-Truk and went to the base of the tree. With a few heavy clangs of the bar, the nest was dislodged enough for him to reach up and grasp it. The pretty forget-me-not blue eggs nestled together, still warm. They each had tiny brown freckles on them and a pearl sheen which glowed with the promise of new life.

Ogmund broke them.

He broke them one-by-one.

He broke them one-by-one and tipped them into his great gaping mouth.

He swallowed them whole.

In gulps.

Ulf couldn't bear to watch.

The Big Man returned to his comfy sitting spot and wiped his mouth with the back of his hand. He belched pleasurably.

"That's the one good thing about birds," he announced, to nobody in particular. "Eggsies! Hah!"

Still Ulf didn't speak. He was appalled but didn't know what to say, and there seemed no point in doing so since Ogmund didn't - or wouldn't - understand Troll Talk. He stared down at the pine needles scattered around his feet, coughing occasionally and trying to work things out.

What was he going to do?

He had to get away from here!

He was sure that his Uncle Bogley would not desert him. He also knew that it was likely that he would have told Hildi and Thom. Surely they could do something to save him!

But where were they?

He hadn't heard them calling him. They hadn't come crashing through the undergrowth with Tracker growling and Grimo screeching. He hadn't even seen the mice. Maybe they thought he would be able to escape by himself and were just sitting at home, sipping nettle tea and waiting for him to come trundling up the path. *Maybe* they had forgotten all about him and were getting on with their normal jobs, just like before. Uncle Bogley would be snoozing in his home-cave. Thom would be fishing or mending his nets, chopping wood for their fire or fetching water from the fjord. Hildi would be baking fresh bread or making honey medicines.

The thought of fresh bread and his Auntie's kindness with honey medicine made Ulf's eyes fill up once more. Why did they not come for him?

~~~

It was turning dusk as Hairy Bogley and Thom made their way wearily up the twisting path to Hildi's door. It took just one quick look for Hildi to know that all was not well in the forest. Wisely, she did not bombard them with questions about Ulf, but kissed Thom's tired old face tenderly and patted Hairy Bogley on the shoulders as they slumped in the wooden fireside chairs.

Another night was spent in dismal silence, each deep in thought, if not sleep.

~~~

The days passed slowly. A routine began to emerge both at home and in the forest. Each morning, Thom and Hairy Bogley would make their way through the diminishing woodland to hide, watch and listen. Each day, Ulf would do whatever the Big Man asked of him, gratefully living off scraps tossed to him which he wolfed down before they were trodden into the dirt. Each evening his uncles would return to Hildi; to eat, rest and ponder.

Ideas were beginning to take shape in Thom's mind. At first they were random fleeting thoughts, like individual, discrete colours flashing in the fjord water, but little by little, they were beginning to blend and fall into place like a rainbow. One idea followed another and a possible sequence of events began to develop. By watching and listening, observing the daily pattern of the destroyer in the forest, he was able to predict and plan. Each night he lay awake, working through his thoughts whilst holding Hildi in a reassuring embrace, as she fidgeted and twitched in her unsettled sleep.

~~~

Thom was up early the next morning. It was time for action! He spoke in urgent tones to the others whilst they listened, eyes wide, nodding agreement. Each had a specific job to do and they felt a warmth of togetherness in achieving their common goal.

At last they were going to rescue Ulf!

At last they were going to rescue the forest!

Hairy Bogley took the long climb to his home-cave to collect his roll of wire and the Dyno-Truk door-janglers. Hildi cut bread and cheese, whistling Tracker to her side. He sat there obediently awaiting his training. Thom hurried on his way to Mistig Vorter and his bee hives. They had to act fast now, whilst they understood the Big Man's daily routine and before Ulf gave up all hope.

The fishing net was lying, neatly folded, on the deck of Mistig Vorter. Thom had always taken great care of his nets with craftsman skill, passed down to him from generations of fisher-trolls. This net was no exception. It was a masterpiece of intricate knots and lacings which meant it weighed next to nothing but had a magical strength about it. Thom was renowned for his skill with nets and this was just perfect for the job. Solemnly, he gathered it up in his arms. He had a very different fish to catch!

The scout bees were easy to collect in Hildi's honey jar. They were still busy searching for their new home and had a curiosity about any nooks and crannies they came across. All Thom had to do was choose a likely-looking log and position the jar next to it. The heather honey scent attracted them and they soon buzzed into the opening. In a trice, Thom leapt upon them and the lid was fastened. He took no notice of their frantic wing-beatings or their furious expressions as he retraced his steps to the little dwelling in the forest.

For once in her life, Hildi was formidable. She would take no nonsense from Tracker, no matter how much he drooled over the bread and cheese. It was critical that she should succeed in her task. The two mice watched the performance with mounting interest. Food was involved and their greedy noses began to twitch. Again and again, Hildi placed the lunch parcel on the wooden chair. Over and over. Tracker watched and waited.

"Shtay, Tracker," Hildi warned, one finger pointing at him.

He sunk down low, chin on paws, tail wagging ever so gently. Grimo smirked at the dog's blind obedience.

Waiting, waiting….

"Fetchen! Fetchen, Tracker!"

The command was whispered urgently, without raising her voice, but with absolute control. The mice were incredulous – encouraging the dog to help himself! That wasn't fair!

Tracker had learnt quickly. Without a second's hesitation, he dashed to the chair and grabbed the food between his teeth.

"Runnig! Runnig!" hissed Hildi shooing the dog away from her so that he pelted off down the woodland path, ears flat, tail outstretched, body streamlined. It was only when he reached Thom who was hurrying home that he stopped and dropped his parcel.

"What did he do that for?" gasped Tailo and Scratchen, as they watched from the kitchen window.

Thom smiled as he patted Tracker's head and scratched him under the chin.

This might just work….

~~~

Hairy Bogley, however, was having his doubts. True enough, he had the roll of wire. It hung heavily coiled on one shoulder. Herbie Poshtig was slung over his other shoulder and contained the door-janglers which had been collected from underneath the heavy, flat stone. So far, so good.

It was just that he felt a bit uneasy when he remembered his conversation with Thom that morning.

He may *just* have exaggerated his driving skill a tinsy bit too much.

~~~

hom was up before dawn. The night had seemed endless and he had found sleep elusive, so alive was his mind with urgent planning. By breakfast time, he had collected his ageing queen bee and had placed her gently in a new skep, deep in the forest. The net had been slung, up, out of the way in a tree top with the experienced skill of a practised fisher-troll and Hairy Bogley's wire had been secured.

All was in place.

All was as it should be.

As Thom hastened back to the others, a cold sun rose in the sky making dew drops on wakening flowers sparkle and catching the Great Waterfall's distant splash. The trees, however, were dark, still and silent. No dawn chorus could be heard, as the forest held its breath.

Hairy Bogley arrived soon afterwards, having spent the night back at his home-cave, going over all he knew about driving: starting, moving and stopping. He really didn't want to let the side down and was determined to put on the brave face of a confident driver. He felt quite pleased with himself now and told Thom there would be no problem. What more was there to know? The Dyno-Truk started, moved and stopped. He had seen it often enough when the Big Man drove it. Ogmund used door-janglers of course. The ones with the strange lines on the leather. He and Thom had spotted those whilst spying in the forest. He had just the same ones, safe in Herbie Poshtig.

Start – move – stop.

Nothing to it.

Hairy hitched up his sagging trousers, sniffed and wiped his nose on the end of his sleeve. He grinned reassuringly at Thom and Hildi.

"Vroom, vroom!" he vroomed, steering a steady course around the kitchen table. "Hoo–hoo–hoo!"

A glance at the cuckoo clock told them there was no time to lose. Tracker was whining at the little wooden door, scratching at its base, eager to be off. Hildi joined him and clicked her tongue encouragingly.

"Gooshty doggor, Tracker," she smiled and adjusted her headscarf so it tucked her wispy white hair neatly in place. Tailo and Scratchen tumbled down from the dresser and scrambled up the dog's back to sit at his neck, gripping the fur tightly. Something was definitely up and there was no way *they* were going to miss out on the action, especially if – as they expected – food was involved.

Hairy Bogley patted Herbie Poshtig to check the clinking of the door-janglers and pulled his red hood down well. Thom passed him the honey jar containing the waking scout bees which were beginning to buzz irritably in their glass cage. They needed to be out and about, finding a new site for the swarm. They needed to report to their queen and were anxious to escape. Hairy looked at the contents of the jar with a worried frown.

"Buzzors verisht dedden, Thom," he murmured in a concerned tone. "Im littelor worrisht...."

"Nay, nay, Hairy," reassured Thom, "buzzors helpen oos. Marvellurg buzzors!"

With a last glance around the kitchen as if to impress the homely, comforting scene on their minds, the trolls, dog and mice departed.

To the depths of the forest.

To Ulf.

~~~

The Dyno-Truk rattled along the road carrying Ulf towards another day's back-breaking, limb-tearing labour. The oily engine screamed as it was forced into each gear, causing sudden forward lurches, belching out navy blue smoke. With each jolt, little Ulf repeatedly rubbed his roughened, blistered hands over his torn blue trousers hoping this would make them feel less sore.

It didn't.

His head ached and kept lolling as his eyelids closed against his will. His whole body was crying out for sleep and food and drink. Last night had not been a good night. He had taken a beating from Birna because she expected him to serve Ogmund's meal, having had nothing himself, and he had sneaked a piece of smoked sausage from his plate. He simply couldn't resist it and knew he had to take the risk. Juices ran in his mouth as he thought of it even now. But Birna had seen, leapt out of nowhere with a shriek, dragged him by his troll tail out of the house and chained him by his ankle to the dog kennel for the night. The dog was fed the rest of the sausage in front of starving Ulf who had wept with despair. The few dog biscuits he had found at the back of the kennel were soft and stale but had given him something to put in his aching stomach. This morning, Birna had released him and reluctantly fed him on the kitchen floor with some grey, sticky porridge, leaving the creamy milk and sugar for Ogmund who ate at the table in grim silence.

Now here he was again, facing the remorseless bullying of the Big People, helping them to trash the precious forest.

He had to escape. He had to think of a plan. He shook his pounding head at the hopelessness of it all. He was too exhausted even to think straight.

The Dyno-Truk came to a sudden halt. Ogmund pulled the hand brake on roughly and turned to Ulf.

"Another day, another Krone!" he smirked. "What wealth there is in these trees!"

Ulf stayed slumped in his seat.

"You are a marvel, little troll," continued Ogmund as he opened the door to the Truk. "You are going to help me get rich! Just think how happy you are going to make my Birna!"

At the thought of Ogmund's cruel wife, Ulf curled his lip and scowled. The Big Man roared with laughter.

"What's the matter? Don't you like the thought of making my sweet lady happy? After all she has done for you? All the kindness she has shown you? All the delicious meals she has cooked for you?"

Ulf could listen to this no longer. He stuffed his fingers in his ears and refused to look at his tormentor. This amused Ogmund no end as he leaned over to open the door and push Ulf out on to the muddy ground.

~~~

It was time to take up battle positions. Each member of the rescue party knew their role and had practised it in their heads, willing the plan to work with every hair of their troll tails. Hildi and Tracker, with the Dyno-Truk clearly in their sights, found a stack of fallen tree trunks which offered them hidden secrecy. Tailo and Scratchen sat on top of the logs, keeping watch. The dog could barely control his excitement. His tail thumped on the forest floor and whenever Hildi bent down low to calm him, he slurped at her anxious face with a great pink tongue.

"Shh, mi lovelor Tracker," she whispered, holding one finger to her mouth, "soonig, soonig!"

She settled down next to him, her head in line with his, watching the Truk.

Thom murmured further instruction to Hairy Bogley and then left him, waiting for the signal. Hairy's position was nearer the Truk, but he could be trusted to keep absolutely silent, bogler that he was. The only noise which came from where he crouched was the buzz-buzzing of the scouts, which were increasingly anxious to be with the others. Hairy lifted the jar and peered at them. His approaching nose was magnified to the bees and they saw it as a massive target, dive-bombing – stingers poised - against the glass. Hairy wasn't sure he wanted to let them out at all but reckoned that if he pulled his hood down quickly, right over his head, he should be safe. All he had to do was wait for the signal from Thom and then act!

Thom cast a worried look at Ulf. He looked as if he wouldn't last another day in the forest. If this plan didn't work today, there might not be another chance. He hurried in a wide circle around where Ogmund was working and found the trees with net and wire. With firm twists, he checked the wire was straight and attached strongly between the two pines. He then shimmied up the tree which held his net and overhung the trip wire. From his position he could survey the scene below with clarity. With luck, the plan would unfold before his very eyes and he would be able to orchestrate each event like the director of a theatre. But there would be no chance of a second performance.

Time passed slowly.

Minute by minute.

Each minute like an hour.

Ulf struggled to drag and lift logs to the Truk.

Ogmund grunted as he used his great saw and ropes.

Tracker watched eagerly, ears cocked.

Hildi kept tight hold of his collar and listened intently.

Hairy Bogley worried about bees and keys.

At last, after what seemed an age, the Big Man dropped his saw to the ground and threw back his head, stretching arms and rotating shoulders to relieve the muscle strain. He mopped his sweating brow with the back of one calloused hand and glowered at Ulf.

"Hey, you!" he bellowed.

Ulf stopped in his tracks, dropping the log he was heaving with a shuddering gasp.

"Worker-troll!" Ogmund shouted over to him. "You seem to have forgotten your worker-troll duties!"

Thom sat up straight in the tree. His eyes searched for Hairy Bogley and sent the low hoot signal. Bogley quickly lifted the lid of the scout bees' prison and released them into the pine-scented air. He hurriedly pulled his floppy hood down over his face and held it tight around his neck. He listened as the bees circled madly, dizzy from their incessant jarbuzzings, and then heard them zoom off in the direction of the new skep to locate the queen.

"Did you hear me, little squirt?" Ogmund continued to snarl. "What should you be doing now?"

Ulf sulked at the ground and kicked the mud with one hairy foot. He knew exactly what he should be doing now. But he was *so* sick of doing it. And *so* tired. And *so* hungry.

Thom watched, silently praying for enough time. He heard the scout bees returning, having found their queen. They jetted past him in his tree and shot off in the direction of the swarm. They were wild and frantic, needing to relocate and settle the workers in their new resting spot. They were under royal orders! Thom nodded with a grim smile.

Just so.

Ogmund strode over to Ulf and looked down at him.

"Well?" he questioned.

"Yo, yo," the sad little troll nodded.

"Yo-yo?" queried his captor, with a sneer. "Yo-yo? You haven't time to be *playing* around, you know-know!" He chuckled to himself. "Now, if you know-know what's good for you, you just go-go to the Truk and," he bent down low, close to Ulf's left ear, "**GET MY LUNCH!**"

Ulf fell to the floor of the forest with fright.

Enough.

Thom whistled a high-pitched clear whistle and Tracker was released.

The game was on.

Just as Ogmund turned to scour the trees with narrowed eyes to find the source of the strange noise, the dog shot out from the undergrowth. His nose had already tracked the stench of egg sandwiches and he pelted towards the open door of the Truk. With one swift dive, the packet of food was in his mouth and, dodging the lunging figure of Ogmund, he made for Thom, following the direction of the whistle he had heard.

"HEY YOU!" Ogmund yelled. "DOG! STOP!"

He made a grab at Tracker as the dog whizzed past. He missed, slipped and lost his footing in the mud. He fell with a resounding splat!

"What the blazes - ?" ranted the Big Man, desperately scrabbling to his feet. He glared at Ulf.

"CATCH THAT HOUND!" he bawled. "SAVE MY LUNCH!"

Ulf did nothing at all.

Except blink twice.

An excited fizz was starting up inside him.

Tracker made off into the forest, heart pounding, towards his master who was now urging him on with whoops and whistles. He flew over the set wire with instinctive accuracy, in one fluid, undetected movement. Ogmund, looking quite deranged with rage, staggered after him, struggling to keep his balance and the pace. His red face was bloated and veins stood out on his neck and forehead as if ready to burst.

"STOP, BLAST YOU, HOUND! HOW – DARE
– YOU – TAKE – MY - "

In an instant, the. panted words were
snatched from him as the trip wire suddenly threw
him to the ground in a breathless heap. Momentarily
dazed at this invisible rugby tackle, he gasped for air,
his black eyes wild and confused.

Thom acted with speed. The net swirled down
from above, entangling Ogmund as he began to
thrash and curse.

"TRUK, Bogley! TRUK!" yelled Thom across
the treetops, his voice echoing and bouncing.

"TRUK, Bogley! TRUK!"

Of course! Heck! Hairy Bogley, who had been
enjoying the entertainment was galvanised into
action. He grabbed Herbie Poshtig and bounded
towards Ulf.

"Onkli Bogley!" Ulf cried in glee, finding his
feet at last and clapping his hands. "Im so happli!
Happli, happli Ulf! Yo, yo Onkli! Kissig, kissig!"

Hairy, with no time for greetings, grabbed his
nephew by the hand and rushed to the Truk door.

"Fastli, Ulf! Fastli!" he urged. "U musten
helpen meer!"

Bundling the little troll into the driver's cab,
Hairy Bogley fumbled about in Herbie Poshtig for the
Truk keys. He had to get going. There wasn't a
moment to lose.

Keys!
Keys!

He thrust his grimy hand around the inside of Herbie Poshtig again.

Keys?

Keys?

Noooo! Where were they? They *had* to be there. He *knew* they were there. He had checked.

But Herbie Poshtig had no keys.

What Herbie Poshtig had was a large hole at the bottom. Hairy looked around in rising panic.

"Janglers! Janglers!" he yelped. "Looki foor janglers!"

From his treetop, Thom was becoming increasingly anxious. The Truk wasn't moving and should be by now. He shot a glance down to the bottom of the tree where Ogmund continued to writhe around in the net. It held fast and was tying him up in knots, but for how much longer? This Big Man was strong. And very angry.

"Janglers!" squawked Hairy to Ulf. "Im needen Truk janglers!"

The net suddenly ripped.

A great fat fist burst out and started to tear at the rest. Thom shot a frightened glance over to the Truk. Out of the net came a great black boot. It kicked and jabbed at the binding knots, widening the escape hole.

"Onkli! Looki!" Ulf shouted in sudden excitement.

"*Janglers?*" screeched Hairy Bogley in desperation.

"Nay, Onkli – buzzors!" squeaked Ulf pointing upwards. "Biggy, vildi buzzors!"

It was true. The sky above them had darkened as an enormous swarm of worker bees pulsated through the air. The skep, with their queen, was just the other side of that annoying net; the one which leapt and jumped about so much, blocking their route, threatening the swarm. The bees had had enough. They had to protect their new hive and their beloved queen. No Big Man was going to get in *their* way!

Just as Ogmund finally burst through, he was completely swamped with stingers. They found any uncovered piece of Ogmund flesh and stung and stung and stung.

The Big Man howled and howled and howled.

He staggered across the forest, still dragging Thom's net by one great boot, towards the safety of his Truk – just as Hairy Bogley found some keys - in the ignition.

Turning them, with a great *wurumph!* the engine roared into life and enveloped Ogmund in choking black fumes. He coughed and spluttered, wildly making a grab for the back bumper, but just missed as the Truk jerkily pulled away. The bees immediately buzzed off, away from the smoke, leaving Ogmund with agonizing swellings bumping all over him. He was seething with fury.

Hairy, on the other hand, was feeling quite mad.

Happy mad.

He was actually driving this Truk!

"HOR EXCITIG!" he yelled to a paralysed Ulf.

His white whiskers flew back from his face in the wind which rushed in through the open window, as he careered out of control.

...white whiskers flew back from his face in the wind...

Hurtling wildly.
Thundering.
Bouncing.
Ever onwards.
    Down the hill.
        Towards the fjord.

~~~

gg sandwiches, Tailo decided, had to be The Best. Once the brown paper packaging had been chewed away, the soft bread and squelchy yellow sumptuousness was all his. Well, mostly all his. He cast a bulging, mouth-filled glance at Scratchen who was delicately sniffing around the stolen lunch, still uncertain as to whether to take an exploratory nibble. Tailo hastily swallowed so that he could speak. It wasn't that he was being polite; it was just that he didn't want to risk choking because that would prevent him from finishing it all.

"If you don't fancy Ogmund's grub, just leave it to me," he told Scratchen in a rather sticky sort of voice. "You know I need a greater amount of sustenance than you, so don't force yourself. I will happily take it off your paws."

Scratchen raised a doubtful eyebrow. He drew breath to answer, having thought of a suitably tart reply but was headed off.

"No, don't thank me, *please*!" Tailo continued, eyeing up his next bite. "It really is *no* trouble. I see it as my *duty* to destroy the evidence – after all, we don't want the Big People to know Tracker stole it - and since I have been blessed with a particularly fabulous capacity for eating egg sandwiches, it seems perfectly right and proper that I should relieve you of the *onerous* task."

So saying, he turned back to his feast. Scratchen gave him one of his best, blackest scowls and tried to nip round the other side of the lunch. His nose was twitchy and his teeth were showing. His scratchy claws were at the ready. Tailo knew better than to upset him too much. Scratchen could be a tricky mouse himself at times.

"Of course, I wouldn't want to take *all* the glory for this," he continued hastily. "Tell you what, I'll leave you the crusts! How about that?"

At this, the two mice simultaneously dived into the squashed egg and began to chomp greedily, each trying to outdo the other, budging and pushing to get at the best bits. A small breath of wind caught the torn lunch paper wrapping and sent it tumbling down the forest path. Neither mouse noticed nor cared.

~~~

The same breath of wind caught the red and white checked curtains of Hildi's kitchen and blew a soothing coolness on her hot, anxious face. She had been pacing up and down for what seemed an age now, waiting for the return of all her dear ones. Once she had released Tracker, she had followed her instructions and hastened home. Thom had not wanted her in danger any longer than absolutely necessary. She had carried out her part in the rescue

124

plan without faltering. The dog had been trained, kept calm, released at the right time and she had returned speedily to await the others. Now was the worst part.

The waiting.

The wondering.

The watching by the window.

Grimo had woken from his early afternoon nap. He had planned to go into the forest for a mid-afternoon think but realised the little dwelling was rather quiet. He was delighted to discover that he had Hildi all to himself. He snaked his way through and around her stocky legs, purring and demanding attention. Getting none, he gave Hildi a gentle nip on the ankle. She bent down to stroke the smoky-grey fur with a trembling hand.

"Mi lovelor pussor," she murmured. "Im verisht worrisht. Mi dearigs leftig in foresh, Grimo. Im so sadli!"

The cat seemed to understand and licked the old fingers tenderly. He turned soulful eyes up at Hildi and she knew he would not leave her this afternoon. The forest walk could wait. In one swift, graceful leap, Grimo was up at the window, also gazing down the path for news.

…also gazing down the path for news…

~~~

With a blim-blam! Birna thumped her rolling pin down on to the worktop, knocking all life out of the grey, flattened dough before her, including the house flies caught in its path.

Chewy little black bits, after all.

Flour cascaded in a cloud over the kitchen as she threw it about in abandon, and with great, fat fists, she pummelled the pastry into submission. Her mouth worked as she did so, grinding her rotten teeth against each other. It felt good to work her muscles. She loved bashing with her rolling pin.

She glanced up at the clock on the grimy wall. Soon Ogmund would be home, with that lazy, good-for-nothing worker-troll. Ogmund would be starving for his meal and that horrid little sneak-thief would be expecting some too. Birna stopped bashing to wipe a floury hand across her sweating brow. As if she didn't have enough to do! Feeding an extra mouth was *not* what she wanted. Perhaps tonight the nasty, whining, little squirt could go hungry. After all, he had porridge for his breakfast; what more did he need in a day? She smiled in satisfaction as she thumped the oven door, entombing the grubby, pigeon pie in suffocating heat.

At that moment, Birna heard a strangulated croak from outside. She couldn't quite place the sound and cocked her head on one side to listen more carefully. The strange cry came again. Curiously enough, it sounded rather like the toad she had squashed with one well-aimed boot, the other day. How very odd! Surely it hadn't survived to croak another day?

Once more the noise was made and, to Birna's horror, was combined with a sudden thudding against the door. Taking her rolling pin in one hand and hitching up her skirt with the other, she tip-toed to the entrance of her home and peered through the letter box.

No sign of anyone standing in front of the door.

Still, Birna was *sure* she had heard a gurgling something. Tentatively, she took hold of the door knob and slowly turned it.

"Hello?" she called through the small gap which was revealed to her. "Is someone there? Name yourself! Man or toad?"

There was a retching sound and Birna's blood froze as she made out the words:

"B-i-r-n-a-agggh! It's me! O-o-open the d-d-door and help me!"

As the door was flung wide, the solid, swollen-faced mass that was Ogmund was found slumped on the doorstep.

"Ogmund! Whatever have you done?" Birna cried in alarm. "Get up, you stupid man! You are showing us up! Think of the neighbours!"

Ogmund staggered to his feet, Thom's net still tangling his lower leg, and grappled with the door for support so that he could make his way inside. Birna quickly cast a look to left and right and followed him.

"What has happened to your face?" demanded Birna as soon as her husband hit his sagging chair with a sigh of relief. "Did you cut yourself shaving today? Or have you got some more spots? What have I told you about washing too much? You know it's not good for your skin!"

Ogmund merely groaned and shook his sorry head.

Birna felt exasperated. She simply could not understand what was going on and was frustrated that Ogmund appeared less than willing to tell her. She looked around for Ulf to give some form of explanation, but couldn't see him anywhere.

"TROLL!" she boomed. "Where are you?"

No answer.

"TROLL!" she screeched. "Come out of your hiding place! You know I'll find you!"

No answer.

"Where is the little pest?" she demanded of her husband. "Exactly what have you done with him? Have you left him in the Truk? You know he can't be trusted! And what *is* that net doing dangling around your feet?"

At this, Ogmund groaned even louder. Birna thrust her cross face in front of him.

"ARE YOU GOING TO ANSWER ME?" she bellowed, with a blast of bad breath.

Ogmund raised his sore head and looked at her. With a deep sigh he answered, reluctantly, "Yes, yes, of course."

~~~

By the time Thom reached home, Hildi was frantic with worry. Time and again she had paced the neatly-swept kitchen floor, wringing her tired old hands and talking to Grimo. She had joined him at the kitchen window to stare down the path and search the surrounding trees for any sign of movement. When, at last, she saw Thom's figure emerging from the gloom of the forest, she knew it was bad news.

"Thom!" she called. "Urnli u homerig?"

Thom nodded solemnly.

"Nay Ulf?" questioned Hildi as he came inside, wearily reaching for the cold water he was offered. "Nay Hairy? Nay Tracker? Urnli u?"

Rarely had she seen Thom so dispirited. She listened in growing horror as he explained how the Truk had gone hurtling out of control, with Hairy at the wheel and Ulf clinging on for dear life, down to the fjord. Tracker had dropped the sandwiches as soon as the Big Man had been caught in the net, as he had been trained to, but Thom had not seen anything of him since. The Big Man had escaped in time to follow the Truk and had taken Thom's precious net with him. Hildi shook her head in disbelief that their carefully laid plan had gone so wrong.

No Ulf. No Hairy Bogley. No Tracker. No net.

And one very angry Big Man.

The arrival of the mice did little to cheer the two trolls as they sat in silence, pondering their next move. Scratchen scampered up the path and on to the dresser where he settled down to scritch-scratch before falling asleep in his special corner. Tailo waddled in afterwards and struggled to climb the dresser leg, so Hildi scooped him up and placed him gently next to Scratchen who was twitching in his mouse dreams.

Thom was in turmoil. He knew he should do his best to save Ulf and Hairy, but this was such a risk. There would be a huge fuss at the fjord edge when the Truk splooshed in. There would be all manner of Big People there by now. He could not risk getting caught up in the frenzy. That would not help at all. How would Hildi cope without him? Without any of them? They would just have to sit tight and let events unfold.

The two trolls sighed and held each other close. They had all done their best. Sometimes, life could not be planned out. Unexpected happenings were always just around the corner. They could do nothing more. They wondered how they were going to pass the time. It seemed impossible to put their minds to anything constructive.

Then, a sound.

What was it?

Hildi and Thom held their breath.

Was it really a dog bark?

Surely not.

Hildi pushed free from Thom's comforting embrace to rush towards the open door.

Could it be their own Tracker?

Please let it be!

Another bark to announce an arrival - and another joyous one of greeting - and Tracker pelted up the path, into Hildi's open arms. So ecstatic was he that Hildi was knocked off her feet and ended up on the kitchen floor, half laughing, half crying, but overjoyed to have this crazy, wet bundle of fur jumping all over her!

"Tracker!" she shrieked in delight. "Mi lovelor doggor!"

The mad dog bounced off Hildi and raced to greet Thom who flung his arms around him. Great tongue lickings soaked Thom's face as he tried to calm Tracker's exuberance. The dog took a couple of steps back from them both, stretched out his front paws and shook himself in a giddy flurry. Droplets of fjord water flew all over the room and had the two trolls squealing and covering their heads.

Thom suddenly caught on.

"Vorter, Tracker?" he queried urgently. "Vorter? Hab u fetchen Ulf?"

The dog rushed back to the door, his tail wagging so much it was a blur. The trolls quickly followed.

They never forgot the scene before them.

At last, there was Hairy Bogley. Hairy Bogley, without his beloved red hood and with wet whiskers drooping, slowly making his way towards them. At first, they couldn't see why he was bent over double, but then it became clear. Wonderfully clear!

Ulf was having a piggy-back.

The best piggy-back ride of his life!

Hearing the noise his appearance created, their nephew raised his head and beamed.

"Halloo! Im homerig! Ulf feelen happli, Antoori Hildi! Happli, happli Ulf!" and he waved both his blistered hands in the air, jigging up and down on his Uncle's back. At this, Hairy Bogley gave up and fell face down on to the path, allowing his joyful burden to jump off his back and skip into a haven of love.

~~~

"We'll be fined you know," declared Birna, folding her arms across her chest and scowling at her husband. "The authorities won't let us leave the Truk in the fjord. Think of all the fuss they'll make about oil and diesel and metal in the water. They'll go all namby-pamby about the birds and fish. We'll have to pay for it to be removed. And now, after your spectacular fiasco over some stupid sandwiches, you can't go back into the forest for tree felling, so where are we going to get the money from, eh? Have you thought about that, eh, Ogmund?"

"Yes, yes, of course."

Ogmund wasn't too keen to return to the forest at all after today's events, actually. He thought it best not to say so.

The Big Man looked very small in Birna's eyes. He seemed to have shrivelled since he arrived home. He was certainly not the man she had once thought he was. Fancy a troll getting the better of him! Stealing the Truk, whisking away their worker-troll and ruining their livelihood! Where would they get another worker-troll from? And another Truk?

And there Ogmund sat, daring to feel sorry for himself with that ridiculous net still wound around his ankle.

A thought occurred to her.

A slow, crafty smile began to calm her thunderous face.

The net!

It was obviously a net which belonged to a troll. She pulled it free and examined it for the first time. This net was no ordinary one. Its knottings and plaited criss-crosses were curiously intricate and it was, apart from the hole her great oaf of a husband had made in it, quite magnificent. It was strong, but light in weight. It took up no space in her great paw of a hand, but could be cast over a vast area. Just think what a Bergen fisherman would give for such a net as this!

Sell it. That's what Birna would do! She could sell it to raise the money to retrieve the Truk from its watery grave. Maybe there would be some money left over! All may not yet be lost.

Birna gathered the filmy mesh together. This net was of value. She glanced over at Ogmund who, exhausted, had begun to snore loudly. Other thoughts began to race through her mind. Surely the troll who had made this net would want it back?

Surely the troll who had made this net would *need* it back?

Surely the troll who made this net would come *searching* for it?

Of course, she sniggered, by then it would be sold.

But other nets could be made by a new worker-troll, to sell on.

So when the troll came sneaking back for his beautiful net, she, Birna ... would be waiting...

~~~

Chapter Ten

ith a clanking, rhythmical, grinding noise of metal on stone, the chains fought to heave Ogmund's sunken Truk over boulders and rocks, from the edge of the fjord. The rescue wagon's engine screamed and its wheels skidded, trying to keep a grip, as it hauled the drenched mass out of the sludge. The Big Man sat to one side, head in hands, unable to watch his work-horse being dragged into view. The future looked bleak indeed. How was he now to earn a living, with no Truk and no access to the trees that remained in the forest? He would have to go into Bergen and find work with other Big Men, be paid a pittance and do what someone else told him. It was bad enough having Birna telling him what to do, without it happening at work as well. What a dreadful prospect! All because of a troll and his puny troll friends. Ogmund let out a sigh which sounded more like a moan from his very soul.

Birna was there also, to witness the event. She, unlike her husband, was *not* ready to give in. Trolls were not going to get the better of Birna. Oh no! She was still furious at their situation and, when she saw the dilapidated Truk which finally had been cranked ashore, she became even more determined.

"Just you wait, troll," she muttered under her breath. "Just you wait, mate!"

The Truk seemed to give one last shudder as it settled on dry land and, in so doing, both the doors fell off in unison, with a final clang. The tyres which had any air remaining in them wheezed their last breath and collapsed. The only set of keys was at the bottom of the fjord, the spare ones having been lost a while ago, under mysterious circumstances. This Truk really was not going anywhere, any more.

An iridescent rainbow fish flipped off the sodden driver's seat on to the pebbles below. It glinted in the morning sunshine for a moment as it struggled to reach its watery home, mouth gaping and gasping for life. Birna scowled down at it, took one great booted foot and stamped.

~~~

As the machinery in the fjord clanked, the cups in the trolls' home clinked.

"Clinkoori foresh!" announced Hildi, holding her heather honey and bilberry juice aloft.

"Clinkoori Hairy Bogley!" declared Thom, chinking cups with his dear friend who had snatched Ulf back.

"Clinkoori Tracker! Clinkoori Tracker!" yelped Ulf as the dog danced around the kitchen, loving the attention. The tale of how this faithful hound rescued them had been told four times over. No detail had been left out in the telling. Thom and Hildi heard how he had plunged into the water just after the Truk had taken a dive. They heard how he had swum out to where it had sunk, watching for the bubbles as they rose to the surface. They still shuddered as they heard how he had struggled, with bursting lungs, to locate the open windows where once the wind had rushed in, but now there was only icy water. How he had fought to grab the belt on Ulf's little blue trousers and pull – pull - pull him up.

Choking.

Spluttering.

Gasping for air.

And then how he had gone down into the freezing depths - again and again - to grip Hairy Bogley, white whiskers floating lifelessly.

And how he had not given up.

And how he had not given up.

And how he had *not* given up.

Until Hairy Bogley was lying with Ulf on the rocky shore.

Coughing.

Breathing.

Laughing at the sky.

Tracker had been awarded special dried meat sticks and he drooled ecstatically as they were solemnly placed in his bowl. The mice were congratulated for their look-out positions in the forest, because they had to be praised for something. Scratchen eagerly gathered the offered berries and nuts to hoard in a corner of the dresser but Tailo was a bit too full of egg sandwiches to consider anything other than staying Absolutely Still. He really felt rather sick. In fact, he couldn't speak.

Grimo was not forgotten. Hildi knew he had been a loyal friend and had helped her through some dark moments as they waited for news. He delicately washed his whiskers after having smoked fish and then mewed prettily at the door, so that he could go out and terrorise the forest mice.

When they had all sat down and calmed themselves, Thom spoke softly.

"Looki, Hairy. Biggy Menor nics gooshty. U musten shtop fetchen thingors. Ulf needen happli homerig!"

Hairy Bogley looked uncomfortable. Collecting things from the Big People was all he had ever known. He had spent a life-time doing it. He did no real harm. He was a perfect bogler. In any case, what else would he do with himself? Ulf could still live with him safely. He could be trained in. Hairy absolutely, definitely, couldn't stop bogling because he-

because Ulf -

because - because it -

because it was *fun*!

Thom and Hildi shook their heads in exasperation at the old, whiskery baddie. It was obvious that Ulf adored him. After all, hadn't Hairy Bogley rescued him in a death-defying driving attempt? And, despite being half-drowned, hadn't Hairy Bogley still given his nephew a piggy-back home? And the hermit troll genuinely wanted to share his home-cave with Ulf, which was no small consideration.

~~~

Birna was busy. She had to pack before going to Bergen, to sell the troll net to the highest bidder amongst the fishermen there. Greed and revenge spurred her on. She would set off early the next day, with net and determination. She would return with a small fortune for the exquisite web she now held in her hands. She snorted loudly as she glanced over to the dull heap sitting on the chair. It would be no use sending Ogmund on such a mission. He had no business sense and he was certainly not Mr Dynamic Salesman of the Year. Birna examined the rip made by Ogmund as he had tried to free himself. She was sure she could cobble it together so that part would never be noticed.

Fix the net. Catch the troll.

As her clumsy darning needle jabbed in and out, she smiled to herself as she pictured the future.

~~~

The golden honey glistened as it oozed through Ulf's fingers, delighting him in its sticky sweetness. Droplets gathered and dripped on to the kitchen floor as he gazed, transfixed, at the amber gloop.

"Rubbig littelor handlies, mi dearig," Hildi instructed him gently. "Honig gooshty foor sadli handlies."

Ulf slowly clasped his sore, chapped hands together and squidged the honey between them, making a wonderful slurping noise as he did so. He smiled like a little troddler and licked some of the squeezed drips before they too slipped off his fingers. He loved Hildi's medicines. His hands were feeling soothed already, but perhaps he needed just a little bit more?

Before he had chance to ask, Hairy Bogley was saying his "gooshty borgs" and heading for the door. He knew that Hildi and Thom had things to do and he was keen to prove he could look after Ulf in a responsible manner. With a backwards wave, his nephew's hand firmly clasped in his, Hairy kicked his legs high in the air. Whistling and chuckling, they bogled off down the path.

Thom sighed as he watched them go. He had a feeling they were going to have to keep a very close eye on those two.

"Im mekken netsy, Hildi. Needen fishen foor oos soonig!" he called as he gathered his things together. Whilst Thom had reserve nets, the one he had lost was his favourite and he wanted to replace it as soon as possible. There was no way he would ever try to get his best net back, he knew, and he had fish to catch. The trouble was that a net of such quality would take time and patient fingers. He wasn't even sure he *could* recreate it. It would be many hours of hard work before he had a finished result.

Hildi picked up her packet of seeds. Time for planting. Time for new growth in those bare patches of forest. Hairy Bogley's gift was just what she needed.

~~~

"The troll *will* want his net back, don't you think?"

"Yes, yes, of course."

"So you *do* understand what I want you to do tonight?"

"Yes, yes, of course."

"You'd better get it right, Ogmund. I've not spent the last hour plucking hairs from my chin and putting rollers in and packing for nothing, you know."

"Yes, yes of course."

"I want to be prepared for my trip early tomorrow and so I'm going to bed. I *can* trust you to stay up, can't I?"

"Yes, yes of course."

"Just in case he comes tonight, you understand. I need my beauty sleep."

"Oh yes! Yes, *of course*!"

"And you need to keep guard on my behalf. Just in case. You won't let me down now, will you, Ogmund?"

"Yes, yes of – I mean **NO!**"

~~~

Night falls, so silently.
Like a soft blanket.

Isn't it quiet, Ogmund?
Do you feel cosy, Ogmund?

Lights out in the town.
Homes gently snoozing.

Isn't it dark, Ogmund?
Do you feel peaceful, Ogmund?

Tick – tick - tick.
Shhhhh…

Close your eyes, Ogmund.
You know you want to.

~~~

In the growing dawn, Hairy Bogley and Ulf slept at last. The home-cave had welcomed them back warmly, its gaping mouth a knowing yawn.

Grimo, stretched out along the foot of Hildi and Thom's bed, rolled on to his back and started to purr. As usual, Hildi stirred first. She smiled a gentle troll smile.

"Gooshty morgy, Thom!" she whispered. "Varken oop."

And, in need of some repair but neatly folded, the exquisite net lay on Thom's doorstep.
Waiting.

Hoo–hoo–hoo!

~~~